"Open in the King's—"

The door slammed shut, flipping Stalwart bodily out into the courtyard. He sprawled flat on his back and his head hit the cobbles with a star-spangled crack.

A whistle shrilled. Boots splattered in the filth as Chefney and Demise came charging past. Demise jumped right over him. "Open in the King's name!"

Clang! Clink! Clang! The sound of swords clashing jerked Stalwart out of his daze. He was in a sword fight, flat on his back with boots dancing all around him. He scrambled to his feet. Someone screamed. Someone fell. Someone dodged around him and ran. He grabbed Chefney's fallen sword and reeled a few steps after the fugitive. Old Blades came streaming in from all directions. Everything started to spin. Voices . . . shouting . . .

Stalwart's knees melted under him and then there were three bodies on the ground.

SILVERCLOAK

Book Three
of the King's Daggers

DAVE DUNCAN

AVON BOOKS

An Imprint of HarperCollinsPublishers

Silvercloak

Library of Congress Catalog Card Number: 2001116347
ISBN 0-380-80100-0

First Avon Books edition, 2001

"Will you walk into my parlor?" said the Spider to the Fly,

"'Tis the prettiest little parlor that ever you did spy.

The way into my parlor is up a winding stair,

And I have many curious things to show when you are there."

"Oh, no, no," said the little Fly, "to ask me is in vain,

"For who goes up your winding stair can ne'er come down again."

—MARY HOWITT
"The Spider and the Fly"

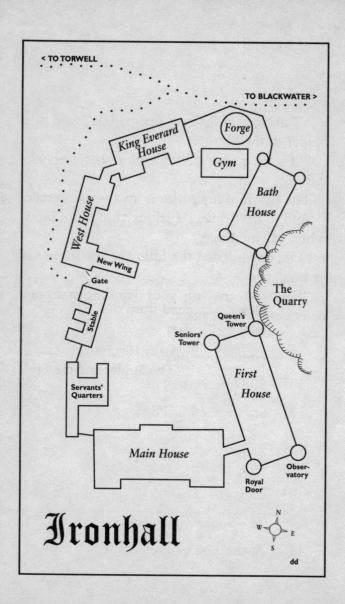

< TO TORWELL

TO BLACKWATER >

Forge

King Everard
House

Gym

Bath
House

West House

New Wing

The
Quarry

Gate

Stable

Queen's
Tower

Seniors'
Tower

Servants'
Quarters

First
House

Main House

Observatory

Royal
Door

Ironhall

N
W   E
S

dd

Contents

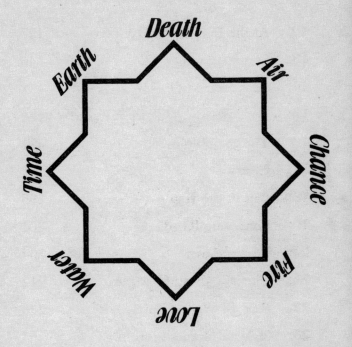

Prologue:
The Monster War

WHEN KING AMBROSE OF CHIVIAL DECIDED TO banish black magic and stop the sale of curses and other such evils, some sorcerers retaliated by trying to kill him. Giant dogs came climbing in his windows; half-human catlike things ambushed him in the forest. Fortunately, he was well protected by the finest swordsmen in the world, the Blades of the Royal Guard, and also by the White Sisters, who were trained to detect magic. While the Guard and the Sisters defended the King, Sir Snake and a group of other daredevils, former guardsmen, attempted to track down the traitors.

By the summer of 368, the Guard was desperate for more Blades to replace those slain in the war. The swordsman school of Ironhall was running boys through their training faster than ever and still could not keep up with the demand.

King Ambrose went there in Eighthmoon and recruited the four most senior candidates, binding them to absolute loyalty in the ancient magical ritual that included a sword stroke through the heart. The next most senior boy, Stalwart, was the best fencer in the school at the time, but everyone agreed he looked far too young to be dressed up as a guardsman. Instead of being bound, therefore, he was secretly enlisted in the Guard and assigned to help Snake. The youngest Blade of all became one of the "Old Blades," but to avoid alerting the traitors' spies, a story was spread that he had run away.

Wart teamed up with Sister Emerald, most junior of the White Sisters, and together they proved so successful at unmasking illegal sorcery that King Ambrose took to referring to them as, *"the King's Daggers."*

(1)

The Snakepit

HAVING SPENT A FEW DAYS WITH HER MOTHER at Peachyard, Emerald headed back to her duties in Greymere Palace in the heart of Grandon. Old Wilf, her mother's coachman, was unfamiliar with the city and took a wrong turning in the maze of narrow streets. Thus he found himself in a shabby alley where there was barely room for the horses to pass and he was in danger of banging his head against upper stories projecting out over the roadway. Street urchins jeered at the rich folks going by; hawkers with barrows cursed as they cleared a path for him. Then his passenger slid open the speaking panel in the roof behind him.

"What's this street called?"

"Sorry, miss——er, Sister I mean. Have you out of here in a jiffy."

"I don't want out of here!" she snapped. She had her mother's temper. "I want you to turn around somewhere and drive back along this exact same street again. And I want to know what its name is."

There was no accounting for the lass, and she would bite his ears off if he argued. Seeing a woman leaning out of an upper window just ahead, Wilf tipped his hat to her and inquired the name of the alley as he went by underneath. "Quirk Row," she said, grinning at his predicament.

He made several right turns and eventually managed to retrace his path along Quirk Row. This time the jeering was louder and some of the gutter brats threw squelchy stuff at him and his highly polished paintwork. He cracked his whip at them, but it did no good.

Another edict from the panel: "Go to Ranulf Square."

The coachman sighed. "Yes, miss, er, Sister." Why couldn't she make her mind up?

He had no trouble finding Ranulf Square, for it was one of the more prestigious parts of Grandon, close by Greymere Palace itself. He enjoyed driving along such wide streets, under the great trees, admiring the fine buildings. His pleasure was short-lived.

"Turn right at this corner!" said the voice of doom at his back. "And right again. Slower . . . Stop here."

"But, Sister!" This street looked very nearly

as unsavory as Quirk Row. The windows were both barred and shuttered, the doors iron studded, and the few people in evidence all looked as if they had just escaped from a jail, or even a tomb. "This is not a good area, miss!"

His protests were ignored. Before he could even dismount to lower the steps for her, Sister Emerald threw open the door. Holding up her skirts, she jumped down. Her white robes looked absurdly out of place in this pesthole. She reached back inside for her steeple hat, which was too tall to be worn in a coach, and settled it expertly on her head.

"Go and wait for me back in Ranulf Square," she called up to him, slamming the coach door. "Er . . . once you've made sure I can get in."

Why would she even want to get in? Spirits knew what might go on behind that sinister façade! But Wilf did as he was bid, watching her run up the steps, waiting until her vigorous pounding of the knocker brought a response. The man who opened the door could not be a servant, for he wore a sword—which usually indicated a gentleman but might not in this neighborhood. He evidently recognized Emerald, for he bowed gracefully and stepped aside to let her vanish into the darkness of the interior.

Whatever would her mother say? Sighing,

Wilf cracked his whip over the team and drove off. He did note the number *10* on the door, and he inquired the name of the road, which turned out to be Amber Street. It meant nothing to him.

It meant nothing to most people.

Most people would not even have realized that these rundown barns backed onto the fine mansions of Ranulf Square. Number 10 Amber Street, for example, was directly behind 17 Ranulf Square, which contained government offices. The brass plates listing these bureaucracies included one saying simply HIS MAJESTY'S COURT OF CONJURY. It was to 17 Ranulf Square that people went to lodge complaints about illegal magic—someone selling curses or love potions or other evils. There the visitors would be interviewed by flunkies whose glassy, fishy stares showed that they were inquisitors, with an enchanted ability to detect falsehoods.

Then files would be opened, depositions taken, reports written. Eventually, if the case seemed worthwhile, a warrant would be issued and the commissioners themselves would raid the elementary. That was when things became exciting. Elementaries might be guarded by watchdogs the size of ponies, doormats that burst into flames underfoot, or other horrors.

The commissioners were all knights in the Loyal and Ancient Order of the King's Blades, former members of the Royal Guard and therefore supremely skilled swordsmen.

In her brief career in the palace, Emerald had learned to avoid red tape at all costs. She knew about 10 Amber Street because she had heard the Blades of the Guard refer to it; they called it the Snakepit. Whatever the brass plates of Ranulf Square might say, the Old Blades' real headquarters was here.

The man who let her in said, "Sister Emerald, this is a wonderful surprise," as if he meant it.

She curtseyed. "My pleasure, Sir Chefney." Chefney was Snake's deputy and had been partly responsible for her hair-raising adventures at Quagmarsh. In spite of that, she liked Chefney. He was unfailingly polite and good-humored.

"What brings you to our humble abode, Sister?" "Humble" was pure flattery. The hallway reeked of mildew and dust, the floors were scuffed and splintery, much of the paneling had warped away from the walls, but originally this had been a gracious, rich-person's residence. Somewhere upstairs feet were stamping and metal clinking as swordsmen kept up their fencing skills.

"Someone is performing an enchantment not

three streets from here. I detected it as my coach went along Quirk Row."

Anyone else except possibly Mother Superior would have countered with, "Are you *sure*?" Emerald might then have made a snippy retort.

Chefney did not ask if Emerald was sure. He did not produce a form for her to fill in nor summon an inquisitor to interrogate her or a notary to witness her testimony. He did not even inquire what a lady was doing driving along Quirk Row. He just said, "In here, please, Sister," very brusquely. As she stepped through the doorway he shouted, "Put away the dice, lads. We've got work to do."

The long room was almost filled by a very large table. The half dozen men standing around it had not been playing dice. They had been rummaging through a wagonload of books and paper, and there were mutters of relief as they turned to greet her. She recognized Sir Snake and Sir Bram and Sir Demise. She was introduced to Sir Rodden, Sir Raptor, Sir Felix . . . and so on.

They were all very much alike, men in their thirties, still trim and athletic, neither very tall nor very short; they all moved like hot oil and their eyes were quick. They looked like older brothers of the Blades of the Royal Guard who strutted around the palace in blue and silver livery and were ever eager to squire a young lady to masques, balls, hay rides, fairs, or a dozen other festivities. The main difference to Emerald was that the Old Blades did not reek of hot iron, which was how she perceived the binding spell on the guardsmen.

The formalities were brief, and then Snake did not even ask her to state her business. He just raised his eyebrows. She knew she might be about to make an epochal fool of herself. What she had sensed might have a very innocent explanation. Then these men would all smile politely and thank her and go back to the important work she had just interrupted.

"My coachman took a wrong turning, into Quirk Row. I detected someone conjuring. I made him go back the same way and noted the house, number 25. There shouldn't be an elementary operating this close to the palace, should there?"

She was meddling in matters that did not directly concern her. Her business was watching over the King in whichever palace happened to be his residence at the time. Correct procedure probably required her to report her suspicions to her supervisor, Mother Petal, who would inform Prioress Alder, who would then write a note to Mother Superior herself, who would pass the word down to old Mother Spinel, who handled relations between the Sisters and the Old Blades—red tape!

Snake did not say, "Oh, that's just the so-and-so Sisters of Healing. They mend peoples' teeth." Or, "That's the Brethren of the Occult Word, where courtiers go for their good-luck charms—they're harmless, so we ignore them."

No, Snake's stringy mustache curled in a leer of great delight. "Absolutely not, my lady!" He was as thin as his namesake and about as trustworthy—utterly loyal to the King, of course. Almost too loyal, because he had been known to use very sneaky-snaky means to achieve his ends, as Emerald well knew. "Bram, the map! Raptor, ring the bell!"

The swordsman nearest the fireplace hauled on a rope. Instead of discreet tinkle in a distant kitchen, this produced a startling clangor out in the hallway, like a fire alarm. The muffled tap of fencers' feet overhead was replaced by sounds of an avalanche on the staircase.

By the time another dozen or so men poured in the door, Emerald was bent over a very grubby and dog-eared chart that Sir Bram had spread out over the table litter. Thick swordsmen's fingers pointed for her.

"Ranulf Square."

"We're here."

"That's Quirk Row."

"What does 'seventy-five' mean?"

"It was about here," she said, when they let her do some pointing of her own. "We came along here and then back this way . . . the elementary's in this building . . . a green door next to an archway . . . about here."

"Aha!" said Snake, and spread himself full-length across the table so he could hold a lens over the tiny scribbles. "Number twenty-five. There's the archway, *there*. Hand me a crayon, someone. Leads through to a mews, or a pump court. So one gets you a thousand there's a back door, even if there aren't any secret passages through the cellars. And there's four ways out of the court, see? That's a fine location for a nest of traitors. What's this 'seventy-five' written here for?"

"Sighting report," said a man in the background, rustling paper. "Must have been recent. Someone claimed he—"

"That was me," said a familiar voice. Stalwart squirmed in through the crowd. "I saw Skuldigger."

Snake sat up on the table and crossed his bony legs. "So you said." He had collected ink stains on his silk hose.

Everyone else made eager *go on!* noises. Skuldigger was the maniac sorcerer genius who had created the chimera monsters. Those had killed many Blades, and more than once endangered the King himself. Skuldigger had escaped at Quagmarsh, but every Blade dreamed of adding Skuldigger's head to the trophies above his fireplace.

"Good chance, Em." Stalwart flashed Emerald a joyful smile. They had not seen each other for several weeks and she had forgotten how boyish he looked, especially when surrounded by men twice his age. If he had grown in the last month, she couldn't detect it. His straw-colored hair was not quite as tumbledown shaggy as before, but still absurdly short.

"Good chance to you, Wart. I hear you're still collecting sorcerers' heads to hang on your wall."

"Oh?" he said casually. "Who told you that?"

"The King. He praised you highly."

His face reddened in anger. "Fat Man has a funny way of showing his gratitude."

She had intended to flatter him in front of the others. She had forgotten how much he wanted to be a *real* Blade, a member of the Royal Guard. Valuable though it was, the undercover work he was doing for Snake seemed to him like cheating, and unworthy.

"*Skuldigger*, guardsman!" Snake snarled. "We're waiting!"

"Er, yes, brother. If I'd had my sword with me, I'd have nailed him to a post and called the watch." Wart was not joking; he was deadly when he had to be. "But I didn't. Saw him on Cupmaker Street, heading toward the palace. Two days ago. I followed him. He turned into Long Bacon Road and I lost him near the Silk Traders' Guildhall." Snake started to speak, but Wart drowned him out. "I'm *certain* he didn't see me. And look on the map— There's an alley there leads into that same pump court!"

"So that was a shortcut for him." Snake leaned over to thump Wart on the shoulder. "He was just going the best way home. Well done!"

"So now do you believe me?"

"Do you think I ever doubted you?" Snake asked in outraged tones, scrambling down off the table in a shower of paper and a couple of writing slates.

"Yes."

"What sort of conjuration?" asked a new voice.

The men cleared a way for a tall, elderly lady in White Sister robes and high hennin. Emerald had met Mother Spinel only once, but knew her reputation as a battleaxe second only to Mother Superior herself. Behind her very upright back she was known as "Sister Spinal."

Emerald struggled to recall the elemental spirits she had detected. "Mostly air, my lady, a trace of fire, I think, and maybe some earth, too . . . I was in a moving carriage. . . ."

Sister Spinal's face had more wrinkles than a basket of walnuts and they all seemed to deepen in disapproval. "Not threatening, then?"

"Um, no, Mother. It gave me no sense of evil."

"Doesn't matter!" Snake snapped. "Unlicensed conjuring near the palace is forbidden and we have a Skuldigger sighting. That's enough. We'll do this the way we did Brandford Priory last week. Sir Dagger, you'll handle the door for us again."

Wart pulled an angry face. "Yes, brother."

"By the time you get there, we'll be in place. If there's no back door, use the front." Snake smirked. "Don't get stepped on!"

Scowling, Wart headed for the door. Emerald noticed grins following him. His earlier exploits had made him a hero, but now the others were treating him as their mascot or water boy. He must hate that.

Snake was barking orders. "Head over there in twos and threes—leisurely stroll, don't hurry, don't dawdle. I want everyone in position when the palace clock chimes three. Chefney, you and Demise take the Quirk archway next to the house itself. Blow your whistle when the kid gets in. They may make a break out the front. Felix and Bram, take Quirk Row on the palace side. Raptor and Grady . . ." When he had assigned everyone he grinned. "Any questions?"

"What if the kid doesn't force the door?"

"I'll bring a pry bar. Two whistles for that, Chef. Any more questions? No? Then go and get your swords wet!"

Laughing, the men began pouring out of the room, almost jamming up in the corridor.

Snake himself paused in the doorway to look back. "Mother, would you be so kind as to alert Master Nicely—soon but not too soon?"

The old lady seemed to draw herself up even taller. "I certainly will do no such thing. You think we Sisters are kitchen scullions to be sent on errands?"

"Ah, well I did try to keep him informed." Snake vanished. Emerald heard him laughing as the outer door slammed.

"Don't they need a search warrant?"

Mother Spinel coughed disapprovingly. "Not

if they can catch them red-handed, and your evidence is good enough for that. Besides, if Sir Snake can just nab Skuldigger, he can count on a royal pardon, no matter what he does. The enchantment you detected—could it have been a language spell?"

"Um, yes! Yes, it could." It could have been several other things, too.

"Interesting." The old lady frowned without explaining why that should be interesting or why she had made such a guess. "And you came straight here, to the Snakepit?"

Emerald braced herself for an ear-roasting tirade on the Importance of Going Through Proper Channels. "Well . . . yes, my lady. I, er . . . Yes."

"Very quick thinking! I commend you. Too many young people today just never seem to use their brains. They have *no* initiative! Where did you leave your coach?"

"Oh! I told the man to wait in Ranulf Square."

Mother Spinel rearranged some wrinkles into what was apparently a smile. "I have to go through to the front office and alert the inquisitors. I don't like Master Nicely any better than Snake does, but he should be told. And also the healers, whom Sir Snake tends to forget until it is too late. I expect you want to see the end of this affair? Why don't we ride over to Quirk Row together and help pick up the pieces?"

"That is most kind of you, my lady." This was turning out to be very interesting afternoon.

(2)

All the King's Men

SIR DAGGER? SPURRED BY FURY, STALWART bounded up two flights of stairs without drawing breath. He was unlucky with names. When he was admitted to Ironhall four years ago, he had chosen to call himself "Stalwart" and promptly been labeled "Wart." That had not bothered him too much, it being so like his original name of Wat, but "stalwart" did not only mean "brave," it also meant "big and strong" and here he was, four years later, just turned seventeen and still a *runt!* Understandably, the Guard had no use for a Sir Stalwart who looked like a puny kid. Now Snake had picked up Ambrose's infantile joke about the King's Daggers, so Stalwart was *"Sir Dagger"* all the time. Big bellylaugh!

He charged into the hot little cubicle that was his personal piece of the world just now. His precious lute stood in a corner and a rickety wicker hamper held all the rest of his worldly goods. He pulled off his baldric and his sword, *Sleight*. He laid her carefully under the bed, then began tearing off his clothes, willfully spraying buttons that he would have to find and sew on again tonight. *What use was a swordsman without a sword?*

Spirits, he was a *good* swordsman! He'd been the best in Ironhall when he was sworn in to the Guard—better than Panther or Orvil or Rufus or Dragon, who had all been senior to him and had been bound that day. It was not because of his swordsmanship that the King had refused to bind him. It was because of his stupid *looks*! He was a better swordsman than most of the Old Blades, even—he could beat Snake with his eyes shut (well, almost). The only men who could outscore him consistently were Chefney and Demise, and they'd both won the King's Cup in their day. Now they were coaching him for next year's tournament, swearing that he was going to come out of nowhere and beat even Deputy Commander Dreadnought, who'd won it for the past two years. One thing Stalwart would not complain about was the fencing instruction he was getting. They worked him to bare bones, day in and day out, but they were making a crack Blade out of him. Chefney said he was already one of the top dozen swordsmen in the *whole world*.

Yet Snake wouldn't let him use his sword in the real fights!

He'd *killed* men, and still they gave him jobs where he couldn't wear his sword.

He threw open the hamper and pulled out a greasy smock, a stinky, tattered thing that left his arms bare and covered the rest of him to the knees. *This* was what he wore these days to serve his King. He'd worn it when the Old Blades raided Brandford Priory, and he'd worn it for three awful days at the Darland Brethren place, working as a kitchen scullion to gather evidence—and bloodcurdling horrible evidence, too. He'd begun his Blade career disguised as a wagon driver, in the Quagmarsh affair, so how could he start complaining now?

It was important work and he'd helped destroy a lot of the King's enemies in the last three months, but he still felt jealous of Orvil and the rest strutting around the palace in their fancy livery. A man needed friends of his own age. All of his were either in the Royal Guard or still back in Ironhall.

He jammed a shapeless cloth hat on his head and slid his feet into wooden shoes. They were surprisingly comfortable and ideal for working in filthy streets and courtyards, but a man couldn't fence in them. He scowled at himself in the mirror. Something wrong? Yes, he was too clean. He ran his fingers along the top of the door and collected a century of dust to smear on his face. He gave his upper lip a double dose and peered closer. There was some faint blond fuzz there, but the dirt didn't really make it any more visible. And now all the world would smell of mouse. Sigh!

Lastly, he took up the feather-stuffed sack he kept in the corner and slung it over his shoulder. It weighed nothing, but back in his days as a minstrel's helper he had learned some miming, so he knew how to make it look heavy. Indistinguishable from hundreds of boys who earned a skimpy living running errands around Grandon, he clattered off down the stairs in his wooden shoes.

Sir Stalwart, member of the Order of the White Star, companion in the Loyal and Ancient Order of the King's Blades, guardsman in the Royal Guard on temporary assignment to the Old Blades, Commissioner of His Majesty's Court of Conjury . . . reporting for duty, SIR!

As Emerald accompanied Mother Spinel through the bewildering interior maze of the Snakepit, she suddenly detected a strong odor of rotting fish. A moment later their way was blocked by a roly-poly man in unusually gaudy clothes—purple hose, silver boots, gold-striped velvet cloak, and a green-and-scarlet jerkin all puffed and piped and slashed. His smile did not go up to his eyes. His bow barely reached down to his shoulders.

"Sister Emerald! I am delighted to make your acquaintance at last, having heard so much about your exploits."

Having never met the man before, Emerald found herself at a loss for words, an unfamiliar sensation. Although he was not wearing the usual black robes and biretta, she knew he was an inquisitor by the stench of the Dark Chamber's conjuration. And there was no mistaking the unwinking fishy stare.

"Senior Inquisitor Nicely," Mother Spinel explained drily, "seeks to impress you with his all-seeing wisdom, but in fact his minions keep watch on the door of the Snakepit. I expect your arms are emblazoned on your coach?"

"My lady," Nicely protested, "you will corrupt the fair damsel with your cynicism." He was not merely hatless but also totally hairless, so that his head resembled a polished wooden ball. His eyes had been painted on as an afterthought.

"There are worse ways of being corrupted," Sister Spinal retorted. "I am surprised that you are not taking part in the raid."

"Raid?" That was the first time Emerald had

seen an inquisitor startled.

"Sir Snake and his merry men are presently storming the illegal elementary at twenty-five Quirk Row."

"I was not informed that there were premises under surveillance at that address."

"Perhaps," Mother Spinel said, with one of her gruesome little smiles, "you should keep closer watch on the enemy and less on your friends."

"Perhaps," Nicely said coldly. He spun around and waddled off the way he had come.

"What is it about inquisitors?" Emerald muttered as they followed.

"They like to make us feel guilty."

"But I have nothing to feel guilty about!"

"To an inquisitor," Mother Spinel said blandly, "that would seem highly suspicious."

The old lady was very effective at getting her way. When they arrived at the musty but grandiose offices of the Court of Conjury, she said, "Why don't you summon your carriage, child, while I roust up a bevy of healers?" and Emerald promptly found herself out on the steps.

There were coaches parked all around Ranulf Square and it took her a moment or two to recognize her mother's on the far side. That was not Wilf's fault, since she had not told him exactly where to wait for her, but now he was deep in gossip with two other coachmen. Street cleaning being a service unknown to the civic fathers of Grandon, and ladies' shoes not being made for walking in mire, Emerald was still frantically waving when Mother Spinel came out to join her on the doorstep.

"Tsk!" the old lady said. She put her head back inside and shouted, "You! Boy!" When an alarmed apprentice appeared, she had Emerald identify her carriage and sent the lad off at a run. Emerald wondered wistfully what would have happened if she had tried that.

But it was fun to see the expression on Wilf's face when he saw the imposing Mother he was to transport, and even more when Emerald ordered him to take them back to 25 Quirk Row.

(3)
Defeat Snatched from the Jaws of Victory

ONE OF IRONHALL'S BASIC LESSONS, POUNDED into every candidate, was *Know your ground.* Wherever a Blade found himself, he owed it to his ward to be familiar with every bush, puddle, and tree—or street, square, and alley, as the case might be. That, the masters said grimly, was often half the battle. Stalwart had spent many hours walking the streets of Grandon. He knew the archway Emerald had mentioned, leading from Quirk Way to the fetid, gloomy courtyard where the locals pumped their water. He even had a vague recollection of the green door she had pinpointed. As Snake had said, there would be a kitchen exit at the rear of the house.

The map had showed four ways into the yard. He went past the Pepper Street entrance, where Sir Julius and Sir Rodden stood, chatting as if they had just met by chance. Julius flashed him a wink. He turned into Nethergate and went along seven houses until he came to Sir Terror and Sir Torquil in a ferocious argument about some fictitious gambling debt. The entrance beside them would do well, because he would cross the full width of the court to reach his destination. If there happened to be guards watching from a rear window—possible, but not probable—they would note the "errand boy's" approach and not be taken by surprise.

Stalwart trudged through the tunnel and across the cobbles, tilted over as if the sack on his shoulder weighed as much as he did. Buildings four or five stories beetled all around, shutting out the light. The air stank of garbage and urine. Two women gossiping beside the pump ignored him, as did some grubby toddlers stalking pigeons, but excitement was drying his throat and twisting knots in his belly. Chefney and Demise stood in the Quirk Row archway ahead of him; neither seemed to look his way, but a casual gesture from Chefney confirmed that the door Stalwart needed was the one next to the corner. It was comforting to know that two of the world's best swordsmen were close at hand to back him up.

The easiest way to open a locked door, of course, was to arm a husky blacksmith or wood-cutter with a sledgehammer and say, "Now!" and then, "Thank you!" For obscure legal reasons, the Crown's lawyers preferred that the door be opened voluntarily. They liked the occupants themselves to admit the King's men, even if the first one in did happen to look like an errand boy.

It had worked at Brandford. A servant girl had opened the door and Stalwart had pushed past her with a shout of "Open in the King's name!" The Old Blades had poured in at his back and most of the enchanters in residence had been arrested while they were still asleep in bed.

If he failed, there were other methods. The inquisitors had a sorcery that would open any door, but the Old Blades did not ask favors of the Dark Chamber unless they absolutely had to. Give those fishy-eyed scorpions an inch and they'd hang you, Snake said. The King had put the Old Blades, not the inquisitors, in charge of the Monster War. Master Nicely and his team were welcome to tidy up later—interrogate prisoners and handle the paperwork.

The door was set back in a shallow alcove. It was made of massive timbers, with a small grille set in it at eye level, and it opened inward, which was good. Still aware that he might be observed, reminding himself that the sack was full of rocks, Stalwart rapped hard with his shoe. He leaned his burden against the wall, to help support it, but in a position where it could be seen through the peephole.

He was just going to kick again when a face peered through the grille . . . a man's face . . . quite young, oddly familiar. . . .

"Carrots!" Stalwart yelled. "Brought your carrots."

"You got the wrong house." Even the voice sounded familiar.

"Twenty-five Quirk Row? Bag o' carrots," Stalwart insisted, speaking as if he were straining to hold up the bag. "Someone here paid five groats for these carrots."

"Well, if they're paid for . . ." A bolt clattered. The door squeaked.

This was the tricky bit. All it needed was one wooden shoe in the door. That mythical black-smith or woodcutter could have just straight-armed the man out of the way, door and all. Stalwart sorely lacked weight, but what counted was not so much weight itself as how you used it. Most people would throw themselves at the middle of a door, which was useless. The trick was to hit the edge, as far from the hinges as possible. He did have surprise on his side.

He leapt. *"Open in the King's—"*

The door slammed shut, flipping him bodily out into the courtyard. He sprawled flat on his back and his head hit the cobbles with a star-spangled crack.

The blacksmith had been on the wrong side. . . .

A whistle shrilled. Boots splattered in the filth as Chefney and Demise came charging past. Demise jumped right over him. "Open in the King's name!"

Clang! Clink! Clang! The sound of swords clashing jerked Stalwart out of his daze. He was in a sword fight, flat on his back with boots dancing all around him. He scrambled to his feet. Someone screamed. Someone fell. Someone dodged around him and ran. He grabbed Chefney's fallen sword and reeled a few steps after the fugitive. Old Blades came streaming in from all directions. Everything started to spin. Voices . . . shouting . . .

Stalwart's knees melted under him and then there were three bodies on the ground.

Hooves clumped, harness jingled, axles squeaked. . . .

"Almost there!" Emerald tried not to sound excited, which she was. Respectable White Sisters must certainly not bounce up and down, either. "I can't detect any sorcery yet, can you, Mother?"

Her companion sniffed disapprovingly. "I detect old meat and fresh sewage. Cats and garlic. But no sorcery."

The coach rattled slowly along as pedestrians grudgingly cleared out of the horses' way. A surprising number of well-dressed young gentlemen had come slumming today, in among the usual shabby residents—Sir Jarvis standing in a shaded doorway, Sir Bram apparently haggling with a pedlar over a string of beads, Sir Raptor and Sir Grady strolling alongside Emerald's carriage. None of them would be visible from number 25.

The coach passed an arch, and Emerald caught a glimpse of a covered walkway and a courtyard beyond. The high note of a whistle stabbed at her ears. Sir Snake appeared from nowhere with Sir Savary and Sir Vermandois beside him, all throwing themselves at the now-familiar green door, beating on it and yelling, "Open in the King's name!"

"Oh, excuse me!" Caught up in the excitement, Emerald grabbed her hat, threw open the carriage door, and jumped out.

Holding up her skirts, ignoring what she might do to her shoes, she ran back to the archway and was almost bowled over by a man who darted out, dodged by her, and vanished into the startled crowd. She caught a whiff of unfamiliar magic, then he was gone.

Snake and four or five others were noisily

forcing the green door, while two more Blades went swarming up the front of the building like cats, already past the overhang of the second story. She raced along the alley, footsteps echoing, into the courtyard where two women and a gang of small children were having screaming hysterics.

The backdoor stood open, emitting sounds of shouting. Two men lay facedown. Sir Torquil was helping Wart to his feet. He was filthy, dazed, unsteady on his feet.

"Take him, Sister!" Torquil said, and she grabbed Wart before he fell. "He's banged his head." Torquil ran into the house after the others.

" . . . 'm a'wright," Wart mumbled.

"You're hurt." She tucked her shoulder under his arm to steady him.

He blinked tears. "Chefney's dead. And Demise."

She glanced down at the two corpses and quickly looked away again. There was very little blood. She had seen dead men before, but this was different; she had liked Chefney—he had regretted the need to be devious, unlike Snake, who enjoyed deception. Demise she had barely known.

It was her fault. She should have minded her own business. She had sent these men here to die. "Let's go inside."

"Couldn't help it," Wart muttered. He walked unsteadily, leaning on her; his face was crumpled with grief. "Unarmed! If I'd had *Sleight* with me I could have helped them." He swallowed hard, as if to banish the quaver in his voice. "Em, Chef and Demise were the best we had!"

"How many traitors were there?"

"Just one." His eyes widened. *"Em, there was only one man!"*

"That's impossible," she said, and realized that that was exactly what he was trying to tell her.

"There isn't a swordsman in the world who could best these two together! . . . 's impossible. . . . I *saw* it!"

The horror in his face frightened her.

The man running . . . "He had magic on him," she said. "I didn't see his face, but I'd know the magic again."

The Old Blades had caught the hated Doctor Skuldigger and his horrible wife, Carmine, the renegade White Sister, who was almost as valuable a catch. They and another dozen men and women were sitting on the floor in a front room in glum silence, their hands on their heads. Sir Bram and Sir Grady stood over them holding swords as if they dearly wanted an excuse to use them. Sounds of boots upstairs suggested that the Blades were still completing their search of the house.

Emerald sat Wart down on a stool to recover. She went off, tracking an odor of sorcery into what was normally a kitchen, where an eight-pointed star had been outlined on the flagstones in red paint. No surprise—an octogram must always be on the ground floor. Earth spirits would ignore the summons if it were upstairs, and air elementals would not go underground.

There she found Sir Snake and Mother Spinel, together with Raptor, Felix, and Julius, who were thumbing through papers on a dresser. The ceiling was so low that Mother Spinel had to stoop, so she was not being Sister Spinal at the moment. She favored Emerald with one of her grim little smiles.

"There you are. A second opinion for the commissioners, if you please, Sister. What was the last enchantment performed in here?"

Emerald closed her eyes for a moment to consider the residual taint of enchantment. Air, fire . . . just what she had sensed in the coach, and there had not been time to perform another conjuration since. "It could have been a memory enhancement, but in that case I'd expect more earth elementals. A language spell does seem most likely, my lady."

"Are you just saying that because I suggested it earlier?"

"No, Mother. But I am not absolutely certain, because this is a very recent octogram, not well seasoned."

Spinel pouted. "Any fool can see that the paint is new." She turned triumphantly to Snake. "A language enchantment has been performed here very recently, within the hour. You see?"

"I don't doubt you, my lady." He had lost his usual cheerful aplomb. He continued to thumb listlessly through a bundle of papers. "So now he can speak perfect Chivian? It doesn't make me feel any better."

The old lady shrugged her narrow shoulders. "Well, you lost him. I'm sure the prisoners have a fair idea of where he's gone and what he looks like. Master Nicely will get the information out of them in short order. You collared Skuldigger! That's what matters."

"What matters is that I lost my two best men! Two very close friends."

The old lady flinched. "I did not know that. I'm sorry."

"No." Snake swung around to peer at Emerald. "What matters is that we almost had

Silvercloak and we lost him. And we never even got a decent look at him! Did you?"

Who was Silvercloak? "A man ran past me, coming out of the alley. . . . He was sheathing his sword as he ran, so he had his head turned away from me. I caught a whiff of sorcery on him, but not strong. I did not get a good look at him."

"I did!" Wart said. He was leaning against the doorjamb, clearly still groggy, although now his pallor suggested fury more than dizziness.

"What did he look like?" Snake demanded.

Wart shrugged. "Very ordinary. Young. Fairish. He seemed familiar, somehow. But I'll know him again when I see him. Who was he?"

Snake threw the papers back on the dresser. "No one knows his real name or where he comes from. He's been called Argènteo or Silbernmantel—Silvercloak."

"A sword for hire," pronounced Master Nicely, mincing in. "The most dangerous assassin in all Eurania, the man who killed the last King of Gevily and the Duke of Doemund. And numerous others. He is deadly, greatly feared, a master of disguise. We at the Office of General Inquiry issued a warning that he was heading for Chivial. In spite of that, you lost him, Sir Snake. His Majesty will not be pleased." Master Nicely was, though.

Snake shot him a look that should have melted all the fat off his bones. "You can have the pleasure of squeezing his plans out of the prisoners. We got Skuldigger."

"A poor second best. You missed the big fish."

"I'd have got him!" Wart shouted. "If I'd had my sword."

"You?" the inquisitor sneered. "When he can take on Chefney and Demise and kill both of them, you think you would have had a chance, boy?"

"He's right, Wart," Snake said. "Not having your sword with you today was probably the luckiest thing that ever happened to you."

(4)

Hidden Agenda

NIGHT CAME EARLY IN TENTHMOON AND SUNSET brought a dreary rain that did nothing to brighten the grim mood in the Snakepit. The Old Blades mourned their dead and wondered what sort of foe could slay their two best single-handed. Magically enhanced swordsmen were not unknown, but the Blades had always held them in contempt. The King's Cup was open to all comers, but only Blades had ever won it.

As miserable as anyone, Stalwart decided to take his throbbing head off to bed right after the evening meal. Then Snake informed him tersely that Lord Roland wanted to see him.

This news raised such interesting possibilities that he went up the stairs three at a time, headache forgotten. He had never been inside Greymere Palace, but he was certain that no visitor could reach the Lord Chancellor's office without being seen by the Royal Guard. Hastily he donned the uniform he had kept so carefully pressed and stored for just such an occasion. It had been made for him on his one and only visit to Nocare, another palace, and he had worn it only once, at a private supper with the King. He was delighted to discover that the jerkin had become tight across the shoulders. The sleeves were too short, the hose too tight. He was making progress! He added the four-pointed diamond brooch that marked him as a member of the White Star, the senior order of chivalry in the land. He had never had a chance to flaunt that in public, either. Just wait until Orvil and the rest of the lads saw that!

When he trotted back downstairs, Snake's only comment was a sardonically raised eyebrow. Under his arm he carried two sheathed swords, undoubtedly Chefney's *Pacifier* and Demise's *Chill*. He was wearing full court dress—resplendent, grandiose, and enormously expensive—and notably a star whose *six* points meant he was an officer in the order. Everyone knew about that, but even Felix, who was with him, obviously had not known that Stalwart was a member. His eyes widened.

"When did you collect *that* bauble, brother?"

Wart shrugged. "Couple of months ago." What use was an honor nobody ever saw?

"Congratulations! I couldn't keep quiet

about it that long if it were mine."

"King's orders," Stalwart said glumly. He had guessed from Snake's reaction that his hopes of parading star and livery where the Guard would see him were about to be dashed, and he was right. Instead of setting off for the palace, Snake led the way into the back corridors that led through to 17 Ranulf Square. He had not mentioned earlier that this was to be a *secret* meeting.

Emerald, meanwhile, had been hustled back to Greymere to report the afternoon's events directly to Mother Superior, whose obvious displeasure made even the formidable Mother Spinel seem mild and benign.

"*Very* bad news!" she barked. "I cannot assign much of the blame to you, but the consequences may be dire indeed."

The two old ladies then proceeded to cross-examine Emerald at great length on the enchantment she had detected on the killer—mostly fire, some water, and traces of earth and death. There were no greater experts in the Sisterhood than that pair, but neither of them could recall encountering such a spell in the past or guess what it might accomplish. She suspected they did not believe her analysis of the elements involved.

"Well!" Mother Superior concluded, obviously meaning *not well!* "By all accounts, this Silvercloak man is utterly deadly. Inform Mother Petal that from now on you are to be posted in close attendance on His Majesty whenever possible. And if you catch even the *slightest* hint of that sorcery *ever, anywhere,* you are to give the alarm *at once!* Do you understand? Even if you have to scream at the top of your voice in the middle of an ambassadorial reception, you will alert the Blades *instantly!"*

From Emerald's point of view, this was very bad news indeed. Close attendance on the King was always wearing and frequently boring. It involved endless traveling. At this time of year he spent days on end chasing game in the royal forests. Courtiers muttered darkly of cramped and drafty hunting lodges.

Besides, tonight Sir Fury had been going to take her to see a play being acted by the King's Men. Duty came first.

She thanked Mother Superior, curtseyed, and hurried off to assume her new duties.

But that was not to be. She had just changed out of her travel-soiled clothes when she was informed that Lord Chancellor Roland required her presence. She had barely time to write a hasty note to Sir Fury before she and Mother Spinel were rushed away in a carriage, escorted through the rain-filled streets by a dozen Yeomen lancers on white horses. Night was falling.

All the clerks and flunkies had gone home, leaving the offices of the Court of Conjury dark and echoing. The meeting room was a gloomy, deeply shadowed chamber, lit only by the dancing light of candles set on a small table in the center. Two naked swords gleamed there beside them. There were no chairs, because the King believed people sitting down talked too much.

Sir Snake and Sir Felix were already present. Beside them stood a blond young man in Royal Guard livery—Sir Stalwart as Sir Stalwart wanted to be, flaunting his diamond star, a cat's-eye sword slung at his thigh. Emerald smiled at him; he winked and grinned back proudly. Honestly, though, he still looked like a boy dressed up.

A familiar stench of rot warned her who was coming before Master Nicely rolled in, wearing formal black robes and biretta. With him stalked Grand Inquisitor himself, like a gallows taking a stroll. The two of them made an unlikely pair— the squat, tubby Nicely and his enormously tall, elderly superior. The only good thing to be said about Grand Inquisitor was that he made even Nicely seem human.

No one spoke. Inquisitors stared fishily across at Old Blades; Old Blades sneered back at inquisitors. Why was Emerald needed? Her report could hardly be simpler and she could add nothing more to it. She was starting to suspect that there might even be worse things in store than "close attendance upon His Majesty."

The familiar dry odor of hot iron announced the arrival of Blades, in this case Sir Bandit and Sir Dreadnought, who were, respectively, Commander and Deputy Commander of the Guard. Bandit concealed warmth and courtesy behind the bushiest, blackest eyebrows in the realm; Dreadnought was blond and usually brusque. They bowed to the ladies, nodded coldly to the inquisitors, and strolled over to join Snake and his men. Stalwart slapped the pommel of his sword in salute.

"Fiery serpents!" Dreadnought said. "No wonder I can't make the payroll accounts come out even! When were you bound, brother?"

"I'm not." Wart's face had gone wooden in an effort to hide his feelings, but he must be deeply hurt that even the Deputy Commander had not known about the secret guardsman.

"Admitted by special royal edict," Bandit explained.

"I didn't know that was possible!"

"First time for everything. Brother Stalwart has proved amply worthy. He won that ornament at Quagmarsh, which was his doing—and Sister Emerald's."

Dreadnought saluted each of them in turn. "I am impressed!" He was flaunting a diamond star of his own, which he had won by saving the King from a chimera monster. Very few Blades in history had ever been appointed to the White Star—as Wart had explained to Emerald more than once—and all three of those still living were here in the room: Snake, Stalwart, Dreadnought.

"So am I," Bandit said. "That uniform looks a little snug, guardsman!"

Wart lit up like a tree struck by lightning. "*Yes,* Leader! I'll order another tomorrow."

The Commander laughed, not unkindly. "Don't be too hasty. His Majesty is very impressed by the work you're doing with the Old Blades. He wants to keep you under wraps a little longer."

Wart deflated with a sigh. "Yes, Leader."

A click as the door closed turned all eyes to the impressive figure in crimson robes standing there, looking over the company as if counting. When he headed for the table, everyone else bowed, curtseyed, or saluted, as appropriate. Lord Chancellor Roland was another knight in the

Loyal and Ancient Order of the King's Blades, the former Sir Durendal. He wore a cat's-eye sword and a diamond-studded brooch alongside his gold chain of office—an *eight*-pointed star. Emerald had forgotten to count him. He was a full companion in the White Star, the highest rank possible. It went with the job of being the King's first minister, head of the government.

For a moment he stared down in silence at the two swords, shaking his head sadly. No one spoke—Roland had the knack of being the center of any room he was in. Everyone else had become pupils before a teacher.

"I hereby give notice," the Lord Chancellor said, "that these proceedings are Deep Counsel as defined in the Offences Against the Crown Act. That means that any mention of them after the meeting ends is automatically classed as high treason unless you can prove that His Majesty's safety required you to speak. That includes mention to anyone else who was present."

He allowed a moment for that dread pronouncement to sink in.

"Let us begin with a quick review of the facts. Sir Snake, will you outline this afternoon's events?"

Snake spoke swiftly, tersely. He began with Emerald's arrival at the Snakepit, went through to the prisoners being formally assigned to the inquisitors, and then doubled back. "The door was magically booby-trapped. Stalwart is no ox, but none of us could throw him around like a pinch of salt. The felon then slew Demise and Chefney and escaped into Quirk Row. Unfortunately Sir Torquil and Sir—"

"Who saw the killer?" Roland must know the answer; he wanted it to be a matter of record. It was soon established that Stalwart was the only one who would be able to recognize the man again. Torquil, Julius, and the rest had seen only his back as he fled and could not even agree whether he had been left-handed or right-handed—a matter of much concern to swordsmen. Even Emerald, who was now called upon to describe her encounter, had not seen his face.

"Just a young man in a pale-colored cloak and a floppy hat. I would know his magic, again, though. It was unusual—fire and water, mostly."

"A disguise spell?"

"Not like any that I was taught to recognize at Oakendown."

"Young, you said. He moved nimbly, I assume, like a swordsman?"

Emerald hesitated.

"Take your time, Sister," Lord Roland

prompted gently. "If you have more to contribute, we are anxious to hear it."

"There *was* something . . . odd about the way he moved, my lord." She could not place it. "Sir Stalwart said he seemed familiar, and I felt the same."

"Interesting! It might be helpful if you two prepared a list of all the people you have both met on your adventures. That might trigger memories."

The Lord Chancellor paused, and the room waited. Emerald wondered why Wart was looking so almighty pleased with himself all of a sudden. Eventually she worked it out. She was the only Sister who might hope to recognize the notorious assassin by the enchantment he used, and only Wart had glimpsed his face. So Wart, too, was going to be posted in close attendance on the King from now on. His days of undercover work were over and he would be moving his lute to the palace at the close of this meeting.

Roland sighed. "We are dealing with most potent sorcery! I am not without knowledge of fencing myself"—the Blades grinned widely—"and I assure all of you that, even years ago, when I was in my prime, I could not have disposed of Demise and Chefney together like that. So we have two of the King's men slain and an illegal octogram. We can be certain that heads will roll or necks stretch."

"Let us hope that royal blood does not flow!" Master Nicely said. "Had Snake followed proper procedures instead of rushing off in the pursuit of personal reputation, this catastrophe would never have happened."

The temperature in the room shot upward. Snake's bony features flamed red. His hand went to his sword. "It was not my reputation that concerned me, Inquisitor. That is safe enough. It was security."

"You need not shout," Nicely retorted, although Snake had barely raised his voice. "You are accusing someone of treason?"

"Keep personalities out of this!" Lord Roland said. "But if you have charges to bring, Sir Snake, we'd better hear them."

Snake must be in considerable trouble if even his friend Roland was taking that tone with him. Emerald wondered just how angry the King was over the day's events. Oh, *why* had she not minded her own business?

"We know the conspirators have spies at court," Snake growled, glaring at Nicely. "We also know that the Dark Chamber employs more sorcerers than even the Royal College of

Conjury. I suspect that some are not above doing favors for old school friends. Or accepting some of their ill-gotten gold. If we had followed the rule book as you suggest, I'm sure we would have found twenty-five Quirk Row an empty shell."

"You may be sure, but have you evidence to persuade others of your lies and slanders?"

"Yes I do. You take charge of all prisoners. Explain to me why three of the men we arrested today are men we have arrested before? Did they receive royal pardons? Or did they *buy* their release from their jailers?"

The inquisitors' fishy stares gave no clue to what they were thinking. No one liked inquisitors, but very few people dared quarrel with them openly like this. The idea that the Dark Chamber might betray the King was terrifying—who could call it to account?

"Is this true, Grand Inquisitor?" the Chancellor demanded.

The gaunt old man displayed long yellow teeth in what could only loosely be termed a smile. "Five days ago we released several suspects—two who had been arrested at Quagmarsh and three from Bosely Down. There was, in the justices' opinion, insufficient evidence to proceed with their cases."

"Insufficient evidence?" Snake howled. "That is the most—"

"Wait! Continue, Grand Inquisitor."

"Thank you, Excellency. Two of them had agreed to turn King's evidence and we believed they would be reliable informants, since we still have their families in custody . . . for their own safety, of course. The other men were being most carefully tracked."

"You are telling me that you had this nest of traitors under surveillance? You had not informed me of this, nor Sir Snake, apparently. Is His Majesty aware of these double agents of yours?"

After the slightest of hesitations . . . "I did inform him, yes. Verbally. Perhaps hastily, as he was occupied at the time in—"

"I have warned you before, Grand Inquisitor," Lord Roland said sharply, "that your reports are to be made in writing and passed through me. Anything you tell His Grace in conversation you are to write down promptly and submit to me. We shall pursue this matter further tomorrow. If you have been subverting criminals with promises of royal pardons, I shall expect to see your authority to do so. Meanwhile, what have you learned from the prisoners taken today?"

"Little so far. The persons apprehended . . ." Inquisitors' memories were magically enhanced,

and the gaunt old man rattled off a score of
names without hesitation. Emerald recognized
only those of Skuldigger and his wife. "Of course
it took us some time to locate His Majesty and
obtain the royal seal on the necessary warrant.
And the Question is a lengthy conjuration." He
glanced around the circle, peering down at
everyone as if curious to know who shuddered
or grimaced at this mention of the most horrible
of sorceries.

"So far we have used it only on the prisoner
Skuldigger. He had just begun talking when I
left to come here. It will be many days before he
can *stop* talking, of course."

"And what was he saying?" the Chancellor
asked with distaste.

"Much as we surmised, Excellency. The traitor sorcerers, having decided that their efforts to
kill the King by magic were meeting with little
success, banded together to hire the notorious
assassin Silvercloak. He arrived in Grandon in an
Isilondian ship this morning. He was taken to
the hideaway on Quirk Row and made fluent in
Chivian; that was the sorcery the girl detected.
He probably answered the boy's knock on the
door just to practice his new skill."

"And what of his plans?"

"Skuldigger knows nothing of them. Silver-cloak works alone and keeps his methods secret."

"But he works for money," the Chancellor said. "Now we have captured those who hired him, he cannot hope to collect whatever fee he was promised. Surely he will simply give up and go home, back to wherever he came from?"

Again Emerald had the odd impression that Lord Roland was asking questions to which he already knew the answer. So who was he trying to impress?

Again she wondered what she was doing here—and Wart also. They did not belong in an emergency meeting of senior ministers.

Then she wondered if those two questions were somehow related.

Inquisitor Nicely replied. "Only two things are generally known about Silvercloak. One is his reputation. He has never failed. None of his chosen victims has ever survived, and he will not want to make an exception in this case. That would be bad for business. The other open secret is that his agents are the notorious House of Mendaccia in Porta Riacha, the most secretive of bankers. Skuldigger and his fellow conspirators deposited an immense sum of money—two hundred thousand Hyrian ducats—with the

Mendaccia. It will be paid to Silvercloak if His Majesty dies by Long Night."

Emerald calculated, and no doubt everyone else did so also. This was a thirteen-moon year, so there were still almost ten weeks left in it for the killer to earn his blood money.

Lord Roland nodded as if satisfied with the way the script was being followed. "Leader, we must assume that His Grace is in grave peril."

"His Grace is spitting fire!" Bandit said glumly.

"You are taking all possible precautions?"

"All *reasonable* precautions, my lord."

There were persistent rumors that when the monsters started coming in the windows of the royal bedroom on the Night of Dogs, Roland, who had then been Commander Durendal, had locked his sovereign lord in the toilet. But Roland was exceptional; if Bandit tried that he would be beheaded. Emerald knew how disinclined Ambrose was to take precautions or put up with restrictions on his movements. Kings did not hide, he insisted. The Blades grumbled that he had more courage than brains and made their work much harder than it should be, but they loved him for it.

"Are there any additional measures we could take to increase the King's safety?"

"Certainly," said Master Nicely. "The Royal Guard may be adequate protection under normal circumstances, but it is obviously not capable of dealing with the world's most deadly assassin. Today Silvercloak showed he could dispose of two of the highest-ranked Blades with no difficulty whatsoever."

Lord Roland frowned. "What are you suggesting?"

"Dogs. As I have previously informed Your Excellency, we can provide a pack of trained and magically enhanced hounds guaranteed to stop any swordsman. Much more effective guardians."

The Blades and Old Blades all growled angrily. Nicely smirked.

"And the answer remains the same," said the Chancellor sharply. "His Majesty refuses to consider the idea. He will not have monsters eating his Blades, he says."

"Or his inquisitors?" said Felix. "Hard to keep a dog away from carrion."

"Snake, if you cannot keep your man quiet, send him home!"

Coming from the great Durendal, that rebuke was enough to turn Felix's face bone white. The Chancellor went back to business.

"Leader, I hope you are taking especial care that His Grace's plans are never announced in advance?"

"Standard procedure, my lord. Our best defense against assassins is always to prevent them from knowing where His Majesty will be or when he—"

"Ironhall?"

This time the interruption came from Wart. Perhaps he had not meant to speak aloud, because he blushed when everyone turned to stare at him.

"You have a comment, guardsman?" The Chancellor's voice was a stiletto dipped in honey, but even he could not intimidate Wart when he had a bright idea to suggest.

"Ironhall, my lord. Fat M— His Grace has been going down to Ironhall to harvest seniors every two months ever since the Night of Dogs, and he's overdue. It's almost three months since I was, er, not bound." His eyes gleamed. Ironhall rules said that candidates must be bound in order of seniority, so the next man up should still be Wart—assuming the King chose to play by the rules, which kings did not always do.

"An interesting point, brother. It is indeed likely that the King will choose to go to Ironhall in the near future. Right, Leader?"

Frowning, Bandit nodded. "Grand Master reports a good crop ready, and spirits know I can use the men!"

"But if his visit is so predictable—no offense intended, Brother Stalwart—then we must take extra care that his enemies do not take advantage of it."

"My lord!" Sir Dreadnought protested. *"Ironhall?* Surely the King is safer there than anywhere?"

"Mm? What do you think, Master Nicely? You've studied Silvercloak's methods."

The tubby inquisitor pursed his fat lips. "How many people live there?" No inquisitors, of course. Probably no inquisitor had ever set foot in the school.

"It varies. Do you know the present tally, Sir Bandit?"

"One hundred and ten boys just now, my lord. Fifteen masters and about a score of other knights—several of them in their dotage—and roughly as many servants. But everyone there knows everyone else. A stranger would stand out like a full-grown lion. And it's all alone on Starkmoor, leagues from anywhere; an assassin could not hope to escape afterward."

"And the Guard goes there when the King does," Dreadnought added.

"True." The Chancellor turned. "You want to continue this argument, Sir Stalwart?"

Wart blushed even redder. "I apologize, my lord. I spoke without thinking."

Emerald knew that Wart knew there had already been a plot—another plot altogether—to kill King Ambrose on his next visit to Ironhall. He had uncovered it by accident and thwarted it, but only the two of them and Lord Roland were aware of it. Perhaps the King had been told, but almost certainly no one else, even the most important people in this room. Apparently Lord Roland did not consider the information relevant.

"If no one has any other suggestions," he said, "we can adjourn. I remind you again how secret these proceedings are; I charge you all to be especially vigilant in the face of this terrible threat to His Majesty. If you have any suspicions at all, pray do not hesitate to inform me or Commander Bandit."

Emerald glanced around the room and saw her surprise reflected everywhere. Why had this secret meeting been called? It seemed to have achieved nothing. Lord Roland was a very clever man, not the sort to waste people's time to no purpose.

What was he up to?

(5)

Stalwart to the Fore

THE FOLLOWING AFTERNOON STALWART WENT
to the Snakepit fencing room for his usual
workout, but it wasn't the same without
Chefney or Demise. No one else could give him
a fair match. Only Dreadnought and some of the
other crackerjacks in the Royal Guard were in
his class now, and they were off-limits for him.
He had just put away his foil in disgust when
Snake appeared in the doorway and beckoned
him out.

His hat and cloak were damp; he smelled of
wet horse. "I want your warrant, Wart," he said
brusquely.

Stalwart almost said, *What?* like a dummy, but
remembered in time that Blades did not question orders. "Yes, brother."

He scampered up the stairs. His commission
in the Court of Conjury was an imposing piece
of paper bearing the royal seal. It gave him enormous authority. Why was he losing it now? Was
he being discharged from the Old Blades at last?

The attics were silent and deserted—but there was a faint odor of wet horse up there, too. The door to his cubicle was ajar. He had left it closed. Warily, wishing he had a sword with him, he stood back and kicked it wide. A man in nondescript, drab-colored clothes was sitting on his bed. Astonished, Stalwart opened his mouth—

Lord Chancellor Roland said, "Sh! Come in. Leave it open a little so I can keep an eye on the stairs. Sit down."

Bewildered, Stalwart perched on the clothes hamper, hoping it would not collapse under him. The great man was smiling, which was a good sign.

"At a recent meeting I mustn't mention, you made a suggestion I won't describe."

"And was shown my folly in speaking out of turn, my lord."

"No." Lord Chancellors could even grin, apparently. "I apologize for snubbing you. Your idea was brilliant. I didn't expect anyone to see that opportunity. I stamped on you because I didn't want it taken seriously."

Again Stalwart swallowed a *What!?* "Thank you, my lord." Then he realized the implications. "You think there were *traitors*—"

"No." Durendal turned serious. "But the danger to His Majesty is so extreme that I do not intend to take *anyone* into my full confidence. Even honest people can be overheard or speak without thinking. I have a job for you if you think you can handle it."

Stalwart could feel a smile creeping over his face, despite his best efforts to remain solemn. "Identify the killer, my lord?" He was going into the Guard at last!

"No." The Chancellor frowned. "You expect me to set you at the King's elbow to shout if the assassin approaches? You haven't thought it through, Stalwart. Put yourself in Silvercloak's place. He has only nine weeks or so to fulfill his contract. He may have some accomplices we don't know about, but in the end he will act alone, because he always does. Now do you see what you missed?"

"Er . . ." It was very flattering to be asked to give an opinion, and very humiliating to feel so stupid. Lord Roland had the reputation of being as fast with his wits as he was with a sword.

"Where does he begin?" the Chancellor prompted.

"Ah!" *Got it!* "He scouts the ground, of course! He'll watch what the King does, where he goes, how he rides out in public, how he leaves the palace. And if he sees *me* with him all the time—"

"Then he kills you first. Or he finds a way around you. You know his face, but he knows yours, too. Not many errand boys issue commands in the King's name."

"So what do I do instead, my lord?" The hamper under him seemed to sense his excitement, for it creaked alarmingly.

"I want to put you in the front line. No one—absolutely no one, not even Leader or the King—knows about this. You are to turn in your present commission to Snake, but Commander Bandit has agreed to assign you to Chancery for a special duty. Will you take my word for that? We haven't had time to do the paperwork and there probably isn't a proper procedure anyway."

"I am honored to be under your command, Your Excellency." Confidential aide to the great Durendal? This was trust indeed. What man could possibly refuse such an adventure?

"Glad to have you." Roland flipped a leather purse at him. "Expenses."

Stalwart caught it; it was heavy and clinked. He felt the belly thrill of excitement that came at the beginning of a new quest. "For?"

"Hasten over to Sycamore Market and dress yourself as a stableman."

"A gentleman's hand or just a churl?"

The Chancellor chuckled. "How about a

well-paid, well-tipped, assistant hostler who sells his employer's oats out the back door and short-changes the customers? Throw in an extra shirt. You may be gone some time."

At least Stalwart would not be shivering in rags, but he still wasn't going to be a Blade. His disappointment must have shown, because his visitor snapped, "You *do* want to see Chef and Demise avenged, don't you?"

"*Yes,* my lord!"

"I'm offering you first shot at the killer. I want you to catch Silvercloak for me. Do that, my lad—" Lord Roland smiled "—and you'll be a hero to the Blades for the rest of your born days. Now, do you want the job?"

"Yes, my lord!"

"Then head out as soon as you've collected your gear. You can make a few leagues before dark."

"Can I wear my sword?"

"On the journey, yes. Now listen. The King will be going to Ironhall very soon, as you guessed. And despite what Leader and Grand Inquisitor and the King and everyone except you and me think, my guess is that Silvercloak will follow—or even be there waiting."

He paused, waiting for comment. Testing.

"He may go by stagecoach, or he may ride,"

Stalwart said cautiously. "It's too far for a single horse, so if he rides, he will need fresh mounts on the way. And if he goes by coach . . . *Yes!* Either way he'll have to visit posting houses."

The Chancellor was smiling and nodding. "But which posting houses?"

"He's a foreigner. He doesn't know the roads. He may go by coach as far as he can, which means . . . The nearest the stage would take him is . . . Holmgarth? And if he's riding, he'll need a remount after that long stretch from Flaskbury. . . . Yes! Holmgarth, my lord?"

"Very well done! You worked it out faster than I did. It's not quite certain. He may see the danger and take a roundabout route. Because, Brother Stalwart—and remember this always—*Silvercloak is the smartest person you have ever met!* Repeat that to yourself once every hour, twice when you go to bed, and three times when you get up in the morning. *Never* underestimate him! Your life will depend on it. If he does slip up and go by way of Holmgarth—"

"I'll be there?"

Durendal nodded. "You'll be there."

The hamper creaked as Stalwart scrambled to his feet, too excited to stay seated. "When I see him I challenge?"

"No. You're too precious and he's too deadly."

"But—" *Wait for the rest of your orders, stupid.*

"But you won't have the Old Blades to back you up this time. No Royal Guard, no Household Yeomen. I could give you any of those, Stalwart, but if I try hiding a dozen armed men behind hay bales in the stables, the whole town will know. Sure as death, Silvercloak will get word of it somehow. I don't want to scare him away! If he takes fright we'll lose him, and he'll strike at some other time and place."

Stalwart nodded doubtfully. He thought the Chancellor was carrying respect for his enemy to absurd lengths.

"We are laying a trap for the smartest man, remember?"

"Yes, my lord. And the deadliest swordsman. So what do I do if I see him?" *Hit him with a shovel?*

The Chancellor shrugged. "That's up to you. A long time ago the King taught me that when you send a man to do a job, you tell him what you want done and let him work out how to do it. If I try to direct you at this distance I'll get it all wrong. You'll be the man on the spot—you decide what to do."

"I appreciate the trust you place in me, my lord." Unless there was more to come, Stalwart was hopelessly out of his depth.

The great man chuckled and produced a sealed packet. "Take this letter to Sir Tancred in Holmgarth. He's a knight in our order but an old man now—he was Leader back in the reign of Ambrose III. After his stint in the Guard he ran the Holmgarth posting house for many years. His sons and grandsons run it now. He was also the county sheriff until his health began to fail this summer. I'm letting his son try out for the job, so he ought to be eager to show his mettle by helping you."

Sheriffs could call out militia. Stalwart would not be alone.

"Without mentioning Silvercloak by name, I've told Tancred about Chefney and Demise and the danger to the King. I've ordered him to give you any help you want. Work out a plan—and let me know what it is. I want a detailed report from you every day by the eastbound stage, understand? Even if you have nothing new to report."

"Yes, my lord."

"Are you familiar with that posting house?"

"I've been through there a couple of times."

"Very solidly built." Lord Roland smiled. "You'll see what I mean. And stablemen are a tough lot. Organize your reception for Silvercloak so that the moment you see him—*snap!* Just don't let him see you first, or you'll be one more name in the *Litany of Heroes.* And I don't want a dozen dead stableboys, either."

"No, my lord."

"Any questions?"

There must be a million questions. "He may have magic tricks?"

"I'm certain he does."

"I have authority to kill him if necessary?"

"Certainly." Then Lord Roland sighed. "But if you do, for spirits' sake be sure you've got the right man! You can't say 'sorry' if you haven't." He waited for the next question.

Stalwart could not think of a single one, which was frightening. He was probably too stupid to see the difficulties until they were on top of him.

Lord Roland said softly, "This may be the toughest assignment I've ever given anyone. Your record is so impressive that you've earned the right to be lead horse on this one, but if you want me to put an older man in charge to take the heat off you, I'll do that. I won't think any less of you for asking. Knowing your own limitations is not cowardice. And sending a boy to do a man's job isn't smart. Is that what I'm doing?"

Stalwart squared his shoulders, wishing they were just a little broader. "No, my lord. I can handle this. If the killer comes through Holmgarth, I'll get him for you."

(6)

Stalwart at His Post

*Done by my hand at Holmgarth Posthouse,
this 22nd day of Tenthmoon, in the year of
Ranulf, 368.*

With humble salutations . . .

Stalwart dipped his quill in the inkwell and
sighed. He had barely begun his job and the
eastbound stage left in an hour. He was writing
his first report. He would rather duel to the
death any day.

*Pursuant to Your Excellency's instructions, I made
haste to Holmgarth. I arrived late last night. I
gave your warrant to Sir Tancred. The noble
knight offered most gracious aid.*

The old man was frail now, but his mind was
still sharp. He had already retired, for the hour
had been late, and he had looked with deep suspicion on the exhausted juvenile vagabond who
came staggering into his bedchamber, dripping
mud and flaunting a cat's-eye sword. The
moment he finished reading the Chancellor's
letter, though, he had ordered food and drink

for his visitor. He had summoned his two sons
and directed them to do anything the stranger
said, without argument or delay. The elder,
Elred, was courteous and silver-haired, keeper of
the inn adjoining the stable. Sherwin was a
rougher character; he ran the livery business and
was also the county sheriff. Stalwart would be
dealing more with him.

After a solid night's sleep, he was just starting
work, so what more could he possibly put in his
report?

*I can easily observe horsemen arriving in the sta-
bles. But the stagecoach and private carriages
usually stop at the post inn to disembark passengers before entering the yard.*

Perhaps he should not whine about his problems, but he was proud of the solution he had
discovered for this one, and it would show Lord
Roland that he had achieved something already.

*I asked the innkeeper to hire workmen to tear
down and rebuild his porch. This construction
blocks the front entrance to the inn. Now all
traffic will come first into the yard and stop at
the rear door. I most humbly request that your
lordship will approve the expense.*

A simple two-day carpentry job might have
to be dragged out for weeks. If they made Stalwart pay for it out of his Guard wages, he would

be poverty-stricken for the next hundred years.

Another clatter of hooves brought his head up as a two-horse gig clattered and squeaked past his window. The passenger was an elderly, plump woman, but he kept watching until he had a clear view of her driver—Silvercloak would not sneak past *him* disguised as a servant!

Two horsemen rode in, three departed. Another carriage ... The post yard was still shadowed but starting to bustle as the sun came over the walls. Men and boys were walking horses, feeding them, currying them, mucking out stables, wheeling barrows, saddling, harnessing. Their breath showed white in the morning chill, and fresh dung on the paving stones steamed. There had been ice on the water troughs at dawn. A farrier's hammer clinked.

Standing at an important crossroads, Holmgarth was one of the busiest posthouses in all Chivial, employing scores of people. Every day hundreds of horsemen hired remounts there and a dozen coaches changed teams. The King boarded horses there for his couriers and the Blades. As if to demonstrate, a horn blew in the distance and men started running. Moments later a royal courier thundered in past Stalwart's window. By then a horse had been led out and was being saddled up for him. In moments he went galloping out through the archway again. *Show-off!*

Could Silvercloak disguise himself as a courier—or even a *Blade*?

The yard was large enough to hold two stagecoaches and their eight-horse teams. It was shaped like a letter *E*, its east side the back of the inn, and three long alleys leading off to the west, flanked by rows of stalls. There was only one gate and the walls were high, because valuable horses must be well guarded.

In tomorrow's report, I shall describe to your lordship my arrangements for catching the

Sir Stalwart pondered a good way to spell "malefactor" and wrote "felon" instead. He had no idea yet what those arrangements were going to be. The iron-barred window of the cashier's office was right by the yard entrance, designed to give a clear view of anyone trying to sneak a horse out without paying. The cashier on duty was Mistress Gleda, Sherwin's wife—a plump, ferocious-looking woman with a visible mustache and a deep distrust of this upstart boy who had taken over half her worktable. Fortunately she was kept busy handling money and tokens brought to the window. Keeping track of all the horses going in and out must be a huge job.

If she was asked, Stalwart was her nephew,

visiting dear Aunt Gleda.

This seat gave him a clear view of anyone arriving. So far so good. He would certainly see Silvercloak if he came, but putting a collar on him was going to be a lot harder. To sound an alarm—ring a bell, say—would alert the quarry as much as the posse. Then the quarry would either escape again or cause a bloodbath.

Roland had dropped a hint—

As your lordship graciously advised, these stables are built of solid masonry. Any stall could serve as a cell.

But if Silvercloak was so smart, how could he be lured inside and locked in—alone, with no hostage to threaten? The answers would have to wait for tomorrow's report. Lord Roland would understand that there had been no time to write more in this one. Now to sign it and then seal it. Blades used the inscription on their swords as their seals. Stalwart's was ᴟɐᴉǝlS —in mirrorwriting, of course.

The door at his back creaked open, and the office was suddenly full of Sherwin. The Sheriff's well-worn leathers bulged over the largest barrel belly Stalwart had ever met, even larger than the King's. He had the biggest hands, too, and a jet-black beard fit to stuff a pillow. At his back came a rangy man, younger and clean-shaven.

."This here's Norton," the big man growled. "Nephew. Can't find me, talk to him. He'll be your sergeant, like. *This* is Sir Stalwart, Norton." He made that last remark seem surprising.

Stalwart rose and offered a hand to the newcomer, whose horny grip did not crush as it might have done. "Please don't use that title, not ever. My friends call me Wart."

"'Pimple' would be better," said Sherwin, looming over him like a thunderstorm. He had very dark, very glittery eyes. His face—the part visible above the undergrowth—was deeply pitted with old acne scars.

"Looks like you know more about pimples than I do. Glad to have your help, Master Norton."

Norton just nodded, but he had not disapproved of the pimple riposte. Sherwin's wife sniffed in an amused sort of way, and Sherwin showed no offense. Perhaps he had just been testing a little.

"We picked out seventeen men for you," he said, "all good lads in a roughhouse."

"Not outsiders?" Stalwart sat down to show that he was in charge.

"You already said you didn't want outsiders. They all work here. Some all the time, some sometimes. I'm not stupid, sonny."

"Will they keep the secret?"

"I don't *hire* stupids, either. You want all of us on duty every day, all day? King'll pay for that?"

Oh, why, why, why had Stalwart not asked Lord Roland how much money he could spend?

"We'll work something out."

"Work it out with Gleda there. You won't cheat her."

Stalwart held fast to his temper as the fat man sneered down at him over his jungle of beard and mountain of lard.

"I don't cheat anyone."

"And if this killer you want is so dangerous, how much danger money will you pay them?"

"How much do you usually pay them? You're the sheriff, so I'm told. We'll cover costs the way you usually do."

Mistress Gleda uttered a disagreeable snort behind Stalwart's back.

"You want me call the lads in so's you can tell 'em what this outlaw looks like?" her husband demanded. "How're you goin' to tip us off when you see him? What d'we do then?"

These were exactly the questions baffling Stalwart, but he was not about to admit this to his troops. "I'll explain all that later. I must finish this letter first. Then I want to take another walk around."

If he was still stymied at noon, he would have to ask for help.

"Why'd Lord Roland send a boy to catch a dangerous killer?"

Stalwart gave the fat man what he hoped was a cold stare. "Because it takes one to know one, I suppose."

"*You*, Pimple?"

"Me. But I only kill traitors, so you should be safe, shouldn't you?"

Before Sherwin could counter, another coach rumbled past the window and headed for the inn door. But the inn door was some way off, and now there were men and boys and horses everywhere, blocking the view. With a yelp of panic, Stalwart jumped for the door, ran outside, and dodged through the crowd. When he got close enough to see the heraldry on the carriage, he almost fell over a wheelbarrow of horse dung being pushed by a skinny, chilled-looking boy.

An octogram and a waterfall? Those were the arms the King had granted to Emerald after the Nythia adventure—a very rare honor for a woman.

He didn't trip. He just stood and stared with his mouth open as the porter opened the coach door, lowered the steps, and stepped back to let the occupants emerge.

Stalwart had never met Emerald's mother, but he did recognize the woman descending. She was not Emerald's mother.

She was not Silvercloak, either.

Silvercloak would have been less surprising.

And the youth in shabby, ill-fitting clothes shuffling along behind her? Yes, Stalwart knew that face also, although the close-cropped hairstyle was new. Fortunately both newcomers disappeared into the inn without noticing him standing there like a lummox.

How many unexpected tricks did Lord Roland have up his sleeve?

This one was almost unthinkable. She was crazy! Why had she ever let him talk her into *that*?

He wandered back into the cashier's office and flopped down on his stool. Norton and Sherwin had left, fortunately, and Mistress Gleda was dealing with a procession of grooms and customers. Stalwart's report, which he had stupidly left lying there, had been moved and therefore read.

More horsemen trotted into the yard and he craned his neck to watch them go by. He had not, as he had thought earlier, solved even the first of his problems. This window would not let him see everyone who arrived, because the coaches unloaded too far away and the crowd would often block his view. So he was right back at the beginning again.

Except he now owed someone for the cost of the inn's new porch.

He must close his report to Lord Roland. He added one more paragraph.

I respectfully advise your lordship that your gracious lady wife passed through Holmgarth this morning with a companion known to me. I judged it fitting that I not address them.

> *I have the honor to be, etc., your lordship's most humble and obedient servant, Stalwart, companion.*

(7)

The Meat Wagon

EMERALD'S PREVIOUS VISIT TO IRONHALL HAD been made in rain and pitch darkness. She had missed nothing in the way of scenery, for Starkmoor was well named. Under a leaden winter sky the rocky crests of the tors were streaked with snow; thorn and scrub tinted their slopes drab brown; and the tarns in the hollows shone a frigid, rippled gray. The only color anywhere was the sinister, lurid green of bogs. Even cattle were rare, and she had seen no houses for hours. As the coach limped and lurched along the track, with wind whistling through every tiny gap, she huddled her blanket more tightly around her.

Lady Kate noticed the move and pulled a face. "There is snow in the air. I have been expecting it ever since we stopped at Holmgarth. This cold is very unseasonable!"

Why was she complaining? She was muffled all over in a reddish-brown fur robe with matching hat and muffs, so that only her face and boots were visible. She looked as warm as a roasting chestnut, while Emerald felt half naked. Cold drafts played on parts of her that were usually covered: ears, neck, legs.

"I hope Wilf is all right." She had volunteered her mother's coach for the journey because her companion's would certainly be recognized by its heraldry. The old man out there on the box had never been this far from Peachyard in his life before, and he might not have thought to bring warm clothes.

"We're almost there."

Ironhall loomed closer now, grim and black. From this angle it seemed to stand atop a low cliff. It sported a few towers and fake battlements, but it was less like a castle than she had expected. The hard knot of nerves inside her twisted.

"This is absolutely your last chance to back out, Sister." Lord Roland's wife was petite and seemed almost fragile, her golden hair and cornflower-blue eyes as bright as glaze on fine porcelain. Nor did she look old enough to be the mother of two children, one of them a son as tall as herself. Appearances were deceptive, though. Lady Kate was most certainly not fragile. A former White Sister, she thoroughly disapproved of the devious scheme her husband had devised. For three days she had been trying to talk Emerald out of it.

"I will not sacrifice all that hair for nothing, my lady."

Lady Kate pouted her rosebud lips. "You may lose more than that. Blood and teeth, perhaps. A great deal of dignity, certainly." Receiving no answer, she asked suspiciously, "Mother Superior did approve this charade, did she not?"

Three nights ago, after the meeting in Ranulf Square, Lord Roland had offered Emerald a ride back to the palace in his carriage—greatly shocking and offending Mother Spinel by not including her in the invitation. But the hasty private discussion that had followed, as the carriage rattled through the rainy streets, had been his chance to explain his Ironhall plan. Emerald had agreed to play her part. Mother Superior . . . ?

"I'm sure your husband said so."

Kate's eyebrows rose as a warning that Emerald was not the only White Sister who could detect falsehood. "Ha! I'll bet he forgot to tell her until after we'd left Grandon and it was too late for her to object. This is an outrage."

Her efforts to dissuade Emerald were self-defeating, for the dominant elements in Emerald's personality were earth and time, a combination that produced extreme stubbornness. Often in the last three days she had almost lost her nerve; left alone, she would probably have backed out by now. Kate's opposition had helped stiffen her resolve.

"I cannot imagine how even my glib-tongued husband ever persuaded you to make such a fool of yourself, Sister."

"He did find me a challenge, I think. Until he offered me a chance to avenge a man I greatly admired."

"Who?" Kate demanded sharply. "Not more deaths in the Order, I hope!"

Sir Chefney's death was still a state secret, not to be discussed. Fortunately the conversation was interrupted by shouting outside.

"Meat wagon!"

"Make way for the meat wagon!"

"Raw meat coming!"

A dozen or so boys on horses pounded past the coach and took up station ahead of it as a ragged guard of honor, laughing and shouting in a mix of treble and baritone. A carriage arriving at Ironhall could be bringing only one cargo.

These were young, feral males—unpredictable and potentially violent. Emerald had met no boys during her years at Oakendown, and her subsequent life at court could be no preparation for Ironhall. She must expect some unpleasant experiences.

Kate said, "Ha! Some of your new friends. Wanting you to come out and play, no doubt."

Again Emerald was saved from having to answer. As the trail bent close to the compound wall, a surge of elementary power made them both wince.

"Spirits!" Kate cried. "You cannot endure that!"

"It is only the Forge, very local." Already the effect was fading.

"I still think you are completely insane. You met Sir Saxon, you said?"

"Grand Master? Once, my lady."

"What did you think of him?"

"I was not much impressed. To be fair, he was in a difficult position that night. Stalwart was there, baiting him mercilessly. He was armed with his commission from the Court of Conjury and eager to pay off four years' resentment."

"That Stalwart wanted to do so says a lot about the man. Durendal never mentions Saxon at all, and I am sure that is because he dislikes speaking ill of people. A mean little politico. Water and chance, I thought."

That was a question, one White Sister to another.

"I thought so too, my lady."

"An awkward mixture. Makes him moody and capricious."

And untrustworthy. "You know him well?"

"No. He came to court briefly a couple of years ago. I don't expect he will remember me."

Nonsense! More than just an important man's wife, Kate was memorable in her own right. Her dominant virtual element was love, and everyone at court approved of her or even adored her, from King Ambrose down to the lowliest flunky. In the rat-eat-rat world of a palace, that was highly unusual. Nevertheless, her manifest element was fire, and there were tales of people who had crossed her and discovered that the kitten had claws.

More hooves thundered past the carriage window and a man's voice bellowed at the self-appointed honor guard, uttering dire threats of extra hours of stable duties. Screaming with laughter, the boys cantered off and vanished like a cloud of gnats.

"Follow me, master coachman!" the horseman shouted.

The trail divided, the left branch curving around the compound to an arched gateway. In the paved quadrangle within, several dozen boys and men were paired off, jumping back and forth and clattering swords. Voices were calling out comments and instructions. The guide led Wilf and the team around the perimeter, to an archaic building with towers and battlements. There he reined in and dismounted. He wore a sword, but was probably no older than Emerald.

He shouted angrily at some of the younger fencers who had broken off their lessons and come running to inspect the new arrival. "Back to work! All of you! If he's admitted you've got lots of time to pick on him. If he isn't, then he's none of your business. Go, or I report you all to Second!"

They retreated, but not far. Clutching foils and fencing masks, they waited to inspect the visitors. Stray snowflakes swirled in the air.

The boy with the sword called to someone named Lindore to look after the horses. Then he dropped the steps, opened the door, and handed Kate down. "Good chance, mistress." He had recognized that the arms on the coach included no crown or coronet and therefore did not belong to a noble. "Prime Candidate Marlon at your service."

About to make a dignified, ladylike descent after Kate, Emerald recalled her new role and jumped instead. Her overlarge shoes almost betrayed her; she stumbled and recovered. The watching boys hooted and jeered. An applicant who fell flat on his face on the doorstep would not go far in Ironhall.

Marlon smiled doubtfully at her and said, "Good chance," again in a kindly tone. Then he offered his arm to Kate. In an all-male world, a lady was *much* more interesting than yet another boy. "If you would be so kind as to let me guide you, mistress, I'll find Grand Master for you. What name should I tell him?" He was trying out the courtly manners he had been taught.

"Mistress Dragonwife," Kate said sweetly.

"Dragonwife?"

"Exactly."

His eyes gleamed with amusement. "I am sure he will be eager to meet you, Mistress Dragonwife."

Emerald slouched along behind, trying to look surly and dangerous, but feeling a freak. This was not her first experience of wearing male clothing, a ruse the White Sisters found expedient on long journeys. They usually did it in groups, though, and Emerald was very much on her own. She was hoping to masquerade as a teenage boy for several days in a jungle of teenage boys. Neither Oakendown nor royal palaces were adequate preparation for that. What did boys talk about among themselves? What sort of table manners did they have? What did they wear in bed and where did they change? And so on.

Although Kate thoroughly disapproved of Emerald's mission, it was typical of her that she had been unstinting in her help—help with hair, with clothes, and with rehearsing the fictitious life story an imposter must have ready at all times. Emerald's breasts were tightly bound inside a coarse linen shirt and stiff leather doublet. Her jerkin and britches were shabby and several sizes too large for her, like hand-me-downs. She had been impressed with her first sight of herself in a mirror, but now fright and the critical stares of the audience made her feel desperately unconvincing.

"Spirits!" said a childish voice from the gallery. "What's he got in those pants?"

"Blubber!"

"Ham? Two hams?"

Emerald was *not* fat! Although her dominant earth element did make her large boned, her mother kept telling her she was too skinny. But she was female and fully grown. Ironhall would not accept boys older than fifteen and preferred them younger, so few newcomers would be her height yet. Those that were would be built like fishing rods. She was not. She needed a bonier face, more chin, and the hips of an eel.

"Hasn't got a hope," said another.

"Grand Master can't be that desperate."

"Have to keep that one away from the swill."

"Run him up Black Tor and back every morning. . . ."

"Aw, the sopranos will soon sweat it off him. . . ."

Emerald's feet froze to the ground, a giant hand of terror crushed her insides to rock, and a voice that sounded very much like Mother Superior's screamed silently in her ear: *Stop! This is madness! You are crazy!* She stood there, watching Kate's back disappearing through the doorway. The urge to turn and race back to the carriage made her quiver like a violin string. What was she dreaming of? Why was she doing this? Not for fat, blowhard King Ambrose, certainly. No, for Sir Chefney— for his gracious bow, his smile of welcome when she turned up at the Snakepit. She had sent him to Quirk Row to die. *That* was why she was doing this! Revenge, justice!

She stuck out her tongue defiantly at the jeering gutter trash, raised her chin, and marched after Lady Kate and young Marlon into Ironhall.

(8)

The Prettiest Little Parlor

LOW CEILINGS AND TINY WINDOWS MADE THE old building dark and uninviting. Prime escorted the visitors along a corridor and up a stair to a gloomy passage furnished with a single crude bench. He threw open a door.

"If you would be so kind as to wait in here, mistress, I will inform Grand Master of your arrival." He stepped back for Kate. Emerald almost made a serious blunder, but remembered in time to let Marlon precede her. As she shut the door, he gave her a wink and a whispered, "Cheer up. It's not as bad as it looks." He crossed the room and left by another door. She decided she approved of Marlon.

The room was grim enough. Snowflakes drifted in through two windows, barred but unglazed, and the hearth was cold and bare. The only furnishings were a table, two hard chairs, and a bookshelf. Lady Kate inspected one of the chairs carefully for cleanliness before trusting her furs to it. Emerald headed for the other.

"I don't think that one's meant for you, boy."

"Oh, probably not." Emerald went to a window instead, clumping in her absurd shoes. The moor was barely visible through flying snow.

A few moments later, Grand Master entered by the second door. He shut it and advanced, rubbing his hands. "I am Grand—" He stopped. "Lady Kate!" He spared Emerald only a brief glance before twisting his beard into a smile. "By the eight, what brings you to Ironhall, my lady? You come incognito?"

Kate offered a hand to be kissed. "Royal business, Grand Master. Royal monkey business in my opinion. My husband is behind it."

"The Chancellor's skill at politics is as admired as his swordsmanship." His words were not quite a lie, but they were so close that Emerald felt the chill of death elementals. Grand Master was jealous of men more successful than himself. Like all Blades, he was of average height and slender build, yet somehow he seemed small. His cloak, jerkin, and britches were shabby. He bore a cat's-eye sword.

In a sudden flash of memory, he swung around to look at his other visitor. "I know you!"

"I was presented to you as Luke of Peachyard, Grand Master." Emerald did not want to antagonize him, but she had already roused painful memories.

"You were with Stalwart that night!"

"I was traveling with him, but I was present here as an unwilling witness only."

That was not the speech of an adolescent male hellion. Grand Master sat down, looking suspiciously from one visitor to the other. In a typical sudden change of mood, he turned a mawkish smile on Kate. "And now you want to enroll him in Ironhall? Or has Lord Roland some more devious prospect in mind?"

"Much more devious, I fear." She handed him a packet she had been hiding in her muff. "And he has won a free hand from His Majesty."

Grand Master scowled as he recognized the King's privy seal. He broke it to read the letter. Emerald knew it contained a blanket command to follow Lord Roland's instructions. Without that royal edict he would not be bound to do so. Chivalrous orders were under the direct rule of the monarch and no one else.

Sir Saxon folded the paper, his lips pale with anger. "And what instructions does his lordship have for me?"

In silence Kate handed him a second letter, this one bulkier. As he read it, the women exchanged glances. More than the premature winter weather was causing the icy chill in that room. Once he looked up briefly to stare at Emerald. By the time he had finished reading, he was livid with fury.

"*Sister* Emerald?"

"I am."

He threw the letter on the floor. "This is madness! You cannot hope to get away with this deception."

"Of course she can," said Kate, who had been arguing the contrary case for the last three days. "She has fooled you twice."

"For minutes only! Your husband talks of days, perhaps two weeks." He returned his glare to Emerald. "You cannot have the slightest idea what you are letting yourself in for! Ironhall collects sweepings of the gutter—thieves, outlaws, arsonists, even killers. These boys are wild and brutal, rejected by their families, often convicted felons whose only hope of escaping the gallows is to be bound as a Blade. That brings an automatic pardon, because by then we have civilized them."

"I know," Emerald said hoarsely, although what he said was not true of all Blades. Marlon's studied manners might hide a seamy past, but Wart had been a minstrel and tumbler, not a criminal.

"Do you know what happens first?" Grand Master thumped the table. "The newest boy is always just the Brat, without a name, without a friend, fair game for anyone. The juniors' recreation is tormenting and hazing him, because they all had to put up with that in their day, so they think they are entitled to do it to others. It weeds out the weaklings, and often it shocks the others into making a fresh start. They can take pride in having survived the worst the rest can do to them. A girl cannot possibly expect to——"

"Sister Emerald," Kate snapped, "is a courageous and resourceful young woman, who has several times performed incredible feats of clandestine investigation in His Majesty's service."

Grand Master swallowed as if at a loss for words.

"I am not without experience of roughhousing," Emerald protested. "I did have two older brothers."

"*Roughhousing,* girl? Even the smallest of these young thugs is probably stronger than you. When your brothers were adolescents did they ever give their sister a thorough pounding? Get you in a corner and pummel you black and blue, throw you on the ground to kick and stamp you?"

"You permit that?" Kate demanded.

"No, but it happens, my lady. Master of Rituals has to perform a healing on almost every Brat at least once, mending flattened noses or broken ribs. I always understood that White Sisters were unable to tolerate healing magic?"

Kate's eyes widened, as if she had not foreseen that problem. Emerald shivered. She thought she could endure a healing if her injuries were serious enough, but she was not sure.

"Some of us can."

Grand Master bent to snatch up the Chancellor's letter again. "Sister, you *cannot* get away with this hoax! In the bath house? The latrines? You are tall, so you will certainly be challenged to fights. Throwing the Brat in a horse trough is a good start to an evening. Then what? And if the juniors ever have the slightest suspicion, they will have the clothes off you in no time."

"Then what?" Emerald barked, louder than she had intended. As usual, opposition was making her dig in her heels. "Will I be assaulted further?"

He stared down at the letter for a few moments, crackling it, while his face turned red and redder yet. At last he muttered, "I don't know. I think and hope that that will be the end of it. I am guessing, because this has never happened."

"Well, then." She rejected her last chance to escape. "If extreme embarrassment and some bruises are the worst I have to fear, I consider the importance of my duties justifies the risk. Does the Chancellor not explain? I must begin by making sure that no sorcerous devices have been smuggled onto the premises and that no residents have been enchanted."

Kate said, "My husband would not be proposing such drastic measures if he did not have real grounds for concern. How long do you suppose that will take you, Sister?"

"A few hours."

"Till sunset, say? Surely you can guarantee her safety that long, Grand Master! If she is willing to continue the deception after she has been shown around, can you not support her for a few days? Then His Majesty will arrive, and you can present your objections to him in person."

This cunning mention of the King made him scowl. He began reading Lord Roland's letter again. Kate shot a triumphant smile at Emerald, who returned it as best she could.

He soon discovered another grievance. "I am instructed to expect Princess Vasar of Lukirk. Who's she?"

Good question. The name meant nothing to Emerald.

"I have no idea," Kate said airily. "Some

foreign royalty the King wants to impress? Possibly a relative of his betrothed, Princess Dierda of Gevily."

The explanation rang like a tin gong to Emerald. Kate was not good at lying.

Grand Master sighed deeply and folded up the letter. He took a moment to become fatherly, then spoke in sorrow. "Sister Emerald, I beg you to reconsider. Believe me, I have only your own good at heart. I am much older than you are. I have known Ironhall since long before you were born, child, and I assure you that what you propose cannot succeed and will cause you terrible heartache. Consider the inevitable scandal, which may ruin your reputation and standing forever. Even if the urgency of the crisis is as great as Lord Roland believes—which I find hard to credit—why cannot you perform your duties in female clothing? Why this playacting, this mummery?"

"To keep my presence here a complete secret." The Chancellor was certainly carrying security to extremes, but he had explained to Emerald that other governments had set every trap imaginable for the notorious Silvercloak. They had all failed.

"I did not say you must wear the habit of

your Sisterhood. Why not be . . . oh . . . my niece, come visiting?"

Emerald returned the answer Lord Roland had given her. "Because a stranger would be noticed. I would not have easy access to every part of the complex, and because traitors, if any, would either take precautions or simply flee."

"But—"

"Cases of treason may require extraordinary measures," Kate said sharply.

Grand Master flinched. When treason was in the air, no one was safe. He shrugged. "Very well, my lady, Sister . . . under protest, I will do as I am ordered. If we are to keep your identity a secret we must follow the normal procedures exactly, yes?"

"As much as possible, please."

He pulled a bag from a pocket. "Lady Kate, please wait outside while I test the 'boy' for agility."

The test consisted of throwing coins for Emerald to catch. It did not take long. Then she had to crawl around on hands and knees to pick up the ones she had missed, which was all of them.

"If asked," Grand Master said smugly from his

chair, "you had better say you caught six. That is the minimum we ever accept."

"Becoming a Blade is not my ambition, I assure you," Emerald remarked from under the table.

"How fortunate! We rarely waste time teaching the Brat anything until we are sure he will be staying. But some time in the next few days Master of Rapiers will undoubtedly give you a foil and check to see whether you have any native ability."

"Which I don't."

"Not a shred. If you were genuine you would be on your way back over the moor already."

She scrambled to her feet. "Then I will have to twist an ankle, won't I? As an excuse not to fight or play with foils, but nothing so serious that you need perform a healing on me."

His eyes flashed. "Use that tone to a master, boy, and you will regret it."

She reined in her temper. He was in the right, which did not excuse his obvious enjoyment. "I am sorry, Grand Master. It will not occur again." Not until the next time.

"You still wish to proceed with this farce?"

"I do."

"Very well. On your own head be it." He rose and frowned out the window. Snow was still falling, starting to settle. "Mistress Dragonwife had better make haste. I will send a couple of seniors on horses to make sure her driver finds his way off the moor. Wait here."

(9)

Intrepid

EMERALD SHUFFLED BACK TO THE WINDOW. SNOW hid the tors. Close at hand, though, three boys were running—not running *to* anywhere, just running, going in circles, clowning, laughing, shouting as they rejoiced in being young in snow. She could not hope to imitate that behavior.

Kate had fussed a lot about shoes, insisting that a boy of Emerald's height would have feet twice as big, which was why she was now wearing flippers, their toes padded with wool.

"I can't wear these," she had protested. "I will trip over them!"

"Nonsense. You just need practice. And they will remind you never to run unless you absolutely must. Women don't run the way men do."

Behind her a door squeaked. A face peered around it.

It was not a conventional sort of face. It possessed a very snub nose; a huge number of sandy freckles; two large blue eyes encircled by fading yellow and purple bruises; and a puffed, inflamed lip. It had one eyebrow, which was the same coppery red as the tangled hair on the right half of its scalp. The other side had been shaved bald and bore the word "SCUM" in black ink.

"You're *staying*?" he asked squeakily.

"Yes."

He yelled approval: "Yea! *Fiery!*" And walked in. He was about twelve, about shoulder height. His threadbare jerkin and britches were squalid, as if they had been used to wipe out half-empty cook pots. "They said you didn't look very promising material."

"You don't look so hot yourself at the moment."

He scowled. "Watch your mouth! You're the Brat now."

Emerald cursed under her breath. "I'm sorry. I forgot!"

"Call me, 'sir'!"

"Yes, sir." Boxing his ears would have to wait.

"The first thing—" Grand Master said, striding in. He glared when he saw she had company.

"Ah, Brat . . ."

Emerald said, "Yes, Grand Master?"

He pointed. "You are still the Brat."

"*I am?*" the boy howled.

"Until Master of Archives signs you in. Go and find him and choose your name. *Then* the new boy takes over."

The Brat shot Emerald a predatory leer, made even more sinister by his swollen lip. "So he does."

She was sure she could outpummel this one if she had to. If he was alone.

"But you have one more duty. You have to tell him all the rules and show him around."

The kid shrugged offhandedly. "Mm . . . "

"Boy!" Grand Master barked. "I recall twice in the last two weeks when you couldn't find a place I sent you to, and once you gave a note to the wrong master. That really was Wilde's fault, for not training you better, wasn't it?"

"Yes, Grand Master," the Brat agreed, stepping right into the trap.

"So if this new boy can't find his way around, that will be your fault!"

The freak face fell. "But—"

"You arguing, candidate?"

"*No*, Grand Master."

"Very well. I want you to show the new Brat *everything,* understand? Not upstairs in King Everard House, of course; not the servants' quarters, and not the Seniors' Tower, or they'll skin you. But everywhere not off-limits. And see he knows all the masters by sight."

"Yes, Grand Master!"

"And if he gets lost tomorrow, then it will be your fault, and you will be punished!"

"B–but . . . me? I mean, I can take him, but most places I don't know what they're *called*. How do I tell the names?"

"Ask someone, stupid." Grand Master smirked at Emerald. "When you're done, come back here. I will announce your admittance in the hall tonight."

"Yes, Grand Master."

"Off you go, then, *boys.*"

Emerald did not like Grand Master's smirk.

"The Brat can go almost anywhere," Lord Roland had told her, "because he is errand boy. He attends no classes, has no other duties. If I send you there as a visitor, you will attract attention and your movements will be restricted. No one really notices the Brat. Other boys haze him, but Grand Master will be able to protect you from most of that without raising any eyebrows. You'll have to put up with a lot of impudent heckling, I admit. You may find yourself dancing like a chicken or turning a dozen somersaults to order. Can I beg you to endure a few days' humiliation for your King?"

But supposing he had been wrong? Supposing

this water-and-chance Grand Master resented the Chancellor's orders so much that he would not defend her? He had told her what she intended was impossible. He could make his own prophecy come true. Now he was pouting down at the Brat, who was holding out a hand to him. Grand Master fumbled in pockets until he found a small brass disk, which he passed over.

The boy showed it to Emerald as he opened the door. "The token, see? When a master sends you on an errand, get his token. Then you're on business and can't be jostled. Come on!" He went downstairs at a run.

Emerald followed as fast as her shoes would allow. She did not understand Grand Master, but she could guess what the Brat meant by "jostle." "So you're safe as long as you have a token?"

"More or less." He ran along the corridor. There were no witnesses, so she ran after him, grinning down at his absurd, half-bald head. "This is First House," he explained over his shoulder. "The oldest. That room we was in is the flea room. We go up here."

First House was a maze, a warren of stairs and passages. She was never going to learn her way around, but judged it wiser not to say so. The Brat plunged around another corner . . . *Yelp! Curse! Thump! Much louder yelp*. . . . Emerald, following cautiously, discovered her guide sitting on the floor in a litter of books, rubbing a pink, freshly slapped cheek. An older, larger boy loomed over him.

"Stupid brainless swamp thing!" The other boy had a possible mustache on his lip. He wore no sword, but the size of his fists and shoulders said he could be dangerous enough without one. "Pick them up!"

The Brat scrabbled around, collecting the books. He knelt to offer them. "I am truly sorry, Most Exalted and Glorious Candidate Vere."

The other took them. "Give me ten!" He watched as the Brat hastily stretched out and performed ten push-ups, then returned to his knees. "And what is this rubbish?"

Emerald could explain that she was not the Brat yet, but such technicalities were not likely to prove helpful. She knelt beside her guide. "I am to be the next Brat, sir."

"*Sir?* You weren't listening, trash."

"I beg pardon, Most Exalted and Glorious Candidate Vere."

"Better. But I'm tired of that name. *You* will address me as Supreme and Mighty Speaker of Wisdom Vere."

"Yes, Supreme and Mighty Speaker of Wisdom Vere."

"And don't forget it." Vere stalked away around the corner.

The Brat rose and slouched off the opposite way, rubbing his face, muttering words Emerald preferred not to hear. "The rest of the fuzzies are all right," he said. "Vere and Hunter are the only real cesspits. Most of the beardless don't jostle much either."

"Sopranos, fuzzies . . . ?"

"Sopranos, beansprouts, beardless, fuzzies, seniors. Seniors wear swords and don't bother you. The rest you just get to know ranks by seeing where they sit in the hall."

"Does it matter?"

"You call me 'sir'!"

"Yes, sir."

"Until I get my name. Then I'll tell you how to address me."

"Thank you, sir," Emerald said, mentally chalking a scoreboard. "The fuzzies are the ones who shave?"

"Naw! Tremayne shaves, and he's just a soprano. It's fencing that counts. That's why there's so many sopranos just now—Tremayne's such a woodchopper that they won't promote him to beansprout and he's holding up a half dozen." The Brat chuckled. "They make him practice all day and all night!"

"Does Brat–hazing go on all the time, too?"

He shrugged. It was no longer his problem. "Jostling? In the day they're usually kept too busy. It's evenings you need to look out. Good, he's in." He walked through an open door and squeaked, "Sir?"

Without question, this was the archive room, stuffed with scrolls and gigantic books, smelling of dust and leather. The man standing at the writing desk under the window was suitably bookish, with ink stains on his fingers and spectacles perched on the tip of his nose. His mousy hair was almost as untidy as the Brat's half thatch. Had he not been wearing a cat's-eye sword, he could have been a clerk or librarian anywhere. He turned and pouted at his visitors.

"Brat? Ah, two brats! One brat, one candidate. Come to choose your name?"

"Yes, sir, please, sir." Recalling his duties to Emerald the boy added, "This's the record office. He's Master of Archives." He was relaxed now, and excited.

"Where *did* I put the book?" The archivist peered around, muttering. "Oh, *where* did I put the book?" He meant some special book, for books were piled everywhere—on shelves, on the floor, on both stools, along with boxes and heaps of paper. ". . . did I put the *book*?"

"Ah!" He retrieved a very slim volume and handed it to the boy. "Here is every name ever approved. The ones marked with a cross are in use. Those with triangles are available. You can choose any of those. Any other name must be approved by Grand Master and you stay the Brat until it's settled. Take your time. You'll be stuck with it for the rest of your life." He turned to blink doubtfully at Emerald. "How old are you, lad?"

"Fourteen, sir."

"Can you read?"

"Yes, sir."

It was obvious from the Brat's dismay that he could not.

"Good. . . . Anytime you have a spare moment and I'm here you can drop in and start going through the book. They can't jostle you in here."

"Thank you, sir."

"It saves my time in the end. Of course they can wait outside for you." He turned to the Brat. "What sort of name? You want to take a hero's name? Some boys prefer one they can make famous themselves. Or a descriptive name, like 'Vicious,' or 'Lyon'? Trouble with those is that they can get you laughed at or start fights. The King doesn't like them, so you may end up a private Blade and not in the Guard. There's lots of names that don't commit you to anything but sound good—'Walton,' 'Hawley,' or 'Ferrand.'"

"Wanna hero's name," the Brat said firmly. "A Blade in the *Litany*. And a name that means 'brave'!"

"Mm. Well, there's 'Valorous.'"

"Or 'Stalwart'?" Emerald murmured.

Master of Archives coughed. "That one would not be approved. . . . I recall no 'Stalwart' in the *Litany*. We had the story of a Sir Valorous the other night. The one who was tortured to death, remember, but did not betray his ward?"

The Brat seemed unimpressed by that as a way to die. "Have any Sir Viciouses been heroes?"

"Don't believe so. The only Sir Vicious I can recall is the last Grand Master. 'Brave' . . . ?" He fumbled pages. "Yes, there's still a Sir Brave somewhere, although from the look of this ink he must be ancient. I could confirm that. . . . I think 'Gallant' is permitted. Yes. 'Gallant'?"

"Don't like it."

"'Doughty'?" Emerald suggested. She was anxious to begin her guided tour. "'Audacious'?

'Dauntless'? 'Pertinacious'?"

The archivist frowned. She was not behaving like the average fourteen-year-old fiend.

"How about 'Intrepid'?" he said impatiently. "Sir Intrepid is in the *Litany*. A fine lad. He died last spring saving King Ambrose from a chimera monster. Sir Dreadnought killed it. 'Intrepid' means 'without fear.'"

"Intrepid?" The boy tried the sound of it doubtfully.

"It would be a very clever choice. When you're ready to be bound, the King will remember what he owes to the last Sir Intrepid and will want to put you in the Guard." He was looking ahead five years. Emerald would be quite content if King Ambrose were still alive five *days* from now, able to leave Ironhall and take her with him.

The boy hesitated, muttering the word as if frightened he might forget it. "There's really chimera monsters? I thought they was just joshing me."

Emerald had firsthand experience of the horrors, but she let the Blade answer. He told of the giant man-cat attacking the King in the forest, of his three Blades jumping to his defense, of Sir Knollys being disemboweled, of young Sir Intrepid closing with the monster so Sir Dreadnought could get behind it and kill it while it was breaking Intrepid's neck. The Brat was convinced, his eyes stretching ever wider inside their bruises.

"Yea! Wannabe *Intrepid*!"

"Good! Now where did I put the current journal. . . ?"

The name was entered in three different volumes, in one of which the new Intrepid made his mark. It turned out that there had been three Sir Intrepids in the Order and two of them had achieved immortality in the *Litany*.

"There!" Master of Archives said, putting away the quill. "Welcome to the Order, Candidate Intrepid! Report here for reading lessons at first bell tomorrow."

"Reading? But I wanna use a sword!"

"No. No fencing and no horses until you can read and write. Off with you."

The new candidate stamped grumpily out into the corridor, his lopsided mane waving.

"You can give me the token now," Emerald said, following him. "Sir."

He fumbled in his pocket and suddenly remembered. "Kneel when you speak to me, Brat!" He beamed as she obeyed. His eyes were not much above hers, even then. "What were those other 'brave' words you said?"

"'Dauntless'? 'Audacious'? er . . . 'Presump-tuous'?"

"Then you address me as Dauntless, Dacious, Presumchus Intrepid." He handed her the token.

(10)

The Soprano Jungle

IN SPITE OF HIS IGNORANCE AND BRUTAL intentions, there was something likable about Dauntless-Audacious-Presumptuous Intrepid. He had panache, and five years of Ironhall might well turn the snotty little horror into a fine young man. At the moment he was a blatant liar. He lied when he claimed to be thirteen. He lied when he told how he had killed people and reached Ironhall a step ahead of a posse wanting to hang him. When he said that the Brat was supposed to sleep in the sopranos' dorm but would be utterly crazy to try, he was telling the truth. But he lied again when he retrieved his blanket from a spidery nook under a cellar stair and told Emerald that this was a safe place to sleep. Obviously he would lead the rat pack there in search of her that very night—he couldn't wait to start getting his own back for everything he had suffered in the past eleven days. Wise Brats, she concluded, found their own hidey-holes and kept their blankets hidden elsewhere by day.

Intrepid lied about the hazing he had endured, exaggerating it to frighten her. He did admit that he might have brought the worst upon himself by losing his redhead's temper and trying to fight back. He had not yet seen that controlling that temper might be the most important thing he could ever learn and Ironhall had already begun to teach him.

She enjoyed his bubbling happiness. He had been brought to the school as a reject, a failure, but now he had run the gauntlet of Bratdom and would be one of the boys. As Grand Master had said, a little pride could work wonders.

After he had run her all up and down and through the labyrinth of First House—flea room, library, Grand Master's study, record office, guardroom, Observatory, and a dozen other places she might never find again—they went out into the courtyard. Snow was still falling. Treacherous footing had driven the fencers indoors. The only people in sight were boys saddling horses near the gate.

"Them's the stables," Intrepid chirped, pointing that way. "Servant barns, West House, King Everard House. That's the bath house and rose garden. That's the gym. We'll go that way and do

Main House last. Come on." He ran. Emerald did not bother asking what the rose garden was. She could guess.

The school had grown haphazardly over the centuries, in a mishmash of styles. The oldest parts, on the east side, were First House and the one Intrepid had called the bath house, both of which sported corner towers. They, and the curtain wall connecting them, were topped with battlements, so any invading army advancing from that direction would be stopped in its tracks.

Main House was an imposing stone-built edifice, built after fake fortifications had gone out of fashion. The gym was more recent still, and brick. The dormitories to the north and west could have been modern timber-and-plaster tenements stolen off any street in Grandon. The stables and servants' quarters had an ageless rustic look.

Forge and gym were freestanding. The rest of the buildings formed a chain around them, those not actually in contact being linked by stone walls. Other than the stage scenery on the east, none of those were high enough to stop agile youths.

Intrepid did not bother taking her to the bath house. He ran straight to the gym, which was a madhouse of noisy sword practice, much too small for the number of people leaping about in it. He hung around for a few minutes, hoping to be noticed, but everyone was too busy.

"King Everard House!" he said, and took off at a sprint again. He had overlooked the Forge, which was hidden behind the gym. Emerald could hear faint clinking of armorers' hammers. Even more, she could sense its surging elemental power and so was glad to avoid it.

She also wanted to avoid running, and chance smiled on her again before they reached the next building—Intrepid slipped on the snow and sprawled flat. She tried to help him up, but he was too furious to accept aid.

"Let's walk," she said. "A broken wrist wouldn't be a very good way to celebrate your admission."

He snarled at her and marched away, trying to hide a limp.

As they reached King Everard House, a young man trotted out. He stopped and grinned and held out a hand to shake. "Well done! I'm Loring. Who're you?"

Intrepid puffed out his chest. "I'm Candidate *Intrepid*! That means 'without fear.'"

"Fine choice! A great name to live up to. About two weeks?"

"Eleven days."

"Average." He flashed Emerald a stunning smile. "You'll hear of Brats having to stick it out for months, but that's rare. And someone else may turn up tomorrow. Good chance to you!" He strolled off, whistling.

Emerald *definitely* approved of Loring.

"A fuzzy," Intrepid said. "Not much of a swordsman."

"Oh?" she said. Who cared? With that profile he was going to break a thousand hearts when he came to court.

They passed by the lecture rooms in King Everard House. Upstairs was where knights and masters slept, and off-limits. Emerald detected no sorcery, other than a faint, pervasive hint of the binding spell everywhere. West House contained the candidates' dormitories, all suitably named, from "Rabbit" and "Mouse" for the sopranos up to "Lion" for the exalted seniors. They all passed her inspection for magic, if not for housekeeping.

The stables, likewise, were free of sorcery. By the time she and her guide emerged from them, the light was starting to fail and the snow had turned to slush. She learned that her shoes leaked. Three boys came running out of the dusk, pink and sweaty, fresh from the gym, seeing a new Brat as future sport.

First they slapped Intrepid on the back, wrung his hand, and introduced themselves as if they had never met him before—Wilde, Castelaine, and Servian. They praised his choice of name. A couple of hours ago they would have insulted and bullied him. Then they turned to study Emerald. They were all tall enough to make Intrepid look like a child, and Servian was full man-size.

"Oh, yucky!" said one.

"They get worse and worse."

"We'll really have to work hard on this one." Servian was heavyset for a future Blade, and obviously the ringleader. If it came to pummeling, he would flatten her, for the sisters at Oakendown did not teach pugilism. "Brat, I am the Most Magnificent and Glorious and Heroic Candidate Servian. You kneel when I deign to notice you."

"I am extremely sorry, Candidate Servian, but I carry Grand Master's token and must hurry. Some other time."

Servian's dark eyes narrowed and yet gleamed brighter. "We really cannot tolerate this insolence. Since you're new, I'll let you off with six somersaults for calling me by the wrong name and six for not kneeling."

"It's not playtime now. Come, Intrepid."

Intrepid was staring at her openmouthed, uncertain whether to be impressed by her courage or delighted by the prospects. Fortunately she was not the adolescent boy they all thought she was; she was a grown woman of very nearly seventeen, highly trained in her craft, and a veteran of hair-raising adventures with Wart. Her confidence threw them off balance long enough for her to slip past them and walk away. She was shaking—from rage or relief or fright or possibly all of those.

The boys followed—Intrepid almost at her side, but not quite, the other three close behind, kicking slush at her bare legs with every step.

"He gave you orders, Intrepid!" Servian said. "Candidate Intrepid takes orders from the Brat!"

Intrepid squealed in horror. "Do not! I'm doing what Grand Master said!"

"Candidate Intrepid takes orders from the Brat!"

Wilde and Castelaine joined in the chorus.

"Candidate Intrepid takes orders from the Brat!"

"Candidate Intrepid takes orders from the Brat!"

More boys came running.

"Candidate Intrepid takes—"

"*I do not!*" Intrepid screamed, dancing in agony, splashing slush.

"Then you'll have to fight him!" Servian crowed.

Emerald strode on, fists clenched, ears burning.

Intrepid looked up—way up—at the Brat beside him. His face was crumpled in misery. "He don't give me orders! Grand Master said I hadda show him around."

"Candidate Insipid takes orders from the Brat!"

"That's *Intrepid*!"

"Insipid! Insipid! Insipid!"

"Invalid! Invalid! Invalid!" yelled one of the others.

Intrepid howled. "Awright, awright, awright! I'll fight him tonight!"

"Fight tonight!" yelled Servian.

Emerald continued to stride ahead, half soaked now. A dozen chanting tormentors marched behind her, pelting her with soggy snowballs. They were passing the servants' quarters, which were off-limits, heading for Main House, but it seemed a fearfully long way away. She felt a desperate need to run but dared not trust her shoes on the slippery paving.

"Faster!" Servian roared, thumping her in the

middle of her back hard enough to make her stumble. "You're serving Grand Master! Faster!"

Thump! again, but she was ready for it and kept her balance. Forget the risk of falling, he was hurting more! Dared she run with so many witnesses behind her? "Women don't run the way men do," Lady Kate had warned her.

Inspiration exploded inside Emerald's head. ("Faster for Grand Master!" *Thump!*) Lord Roland had asked, "He moved nimbly, I assume, like a swordsman?"

("Faster for Grand Master!" *Thump!*)

She barely noticed the pain. She recalled her answer: "There *was* something odd about the way he moved."

"Faster for Grand Master!"

Thump!

They were all shouting it now: "Faster for Grand Master!"

Thump! Servian's punches were growing steadily harder, all on the same place between her shoulder blades.

And still her mind was far away, remembering the encounter in Quirk Row. Was it possible? Could the deadly Silvercloak be playing the same deception she was? Could the killer actually be a woman? That could explain "his" skill at disguise—she committed her crimes in disguise, and the rest of time everyone looked for the wrong sort of person. It meant Lord Roland was looking for the wrong sort of person right now! So were Wart and Sir Bandit. They must all be warned—

"Faster for Grand Master!" *Thump!*

Emerald spun and swung a haymaker blow at her tormentor. "Shut up, you great lout! I'm trying to think."

Her wild swipe missed, of course—Servian was a hundred times faster than she was. She would never, ever, lay a hand on Servian. But in evading her he stepped on another boy's toe and lost his footing. His legs shot out from under him and he sat down hard, perhaps harder than he ever had.

Splat!

Shower of slush.

The audience howled with joy. Servian came up screaming, intent on massacring the Brat who had so humiliated him. Others grabbed him. It took four of them to force him along as they marched off into the dusk, happily chanting.

"Two fights tonight! Two fights tonight! Two fights . . ."

(11)
At the End of the Day (1)

IT WAS SUNSET BEFORE BUSINESS SLACKENED IN the posthouse yard. Travelers stopped arriving. Weary grooms were settling the last horses in their stalls.

Stalwart had spent all day chasing around in search of a viewpoint from which he could see everyone arriving without being seen himself. He had not found one. If he stayed at the gate, he could not see the coach passengers; at the inn door he might miss solitary horsemen. He was *almost* certain that Silvercloak had not passed through there that day, but could have done nothing to stop him if he had. Baffled, he trudged into the cashier's office and sank wearily onto his stool. Gleda had been sent home to make supper. Sherwin himself was counting the day's take, clinking coins into bags.

"Still no prisoners, Pimple?"

Stalwart shook his head. "I need some advice."

The sheriff looked up mockingly. "Spirits!

You mean you're actually asking for help?"

Stalwart swallowed his pride, like a brick. "Yes, sir."

"Well! About time." The fat man leaned back against the wall. "What do you need to know?"

"Lots of things. Like how to apprehend an armed and extremely dangerous swordsman after I spot him." A sheriff ought to know that much. "I don't want men killed. I'm trying to think of some way of luring him into a horse stall and then—"

Sherwin said a word never heard around court, except sometimes from the King himself. "How good are you with that sword of yours?"

"I'm a Blade."

"How good a Blade?"

"Better than most," Wart said defiantly.

"Are you so?" The Sheriff scratched his great beard. "Why don't I get my trusty quarterstaff and we'll go outside and try a round or two?"

A man his size would move like a pudding, and Stalwart was lightning on wheels. But a rapier was not the best weapon against a quarterstaff, and he lacked the muscle to swing a broadsword. Ironhall warned against quarterstaffs. They were peasants' weapons, not romantic, not impressive. But out-of-doors or wherever there was space, an agile man with a six-foot ash pole was a dangerous opponent, even for a Blade.

"I think it'd be a standoff. I'd stay out of your reach, but you'd be out of mine." Flesh wound versus cracked head.

"And if I had Norton to help? Him and another ten, say?"

Stalwart laughed, feeling one of his clouds lift. "Your men are trained in quarterstaff?"

The dark eyes glinted sardonically. "Every one, sonny. And no one notices a pole or two stacked around a stable yard. You point out your killer to us and he'll have a broken shoulder before he knows what's happening. And a broken leg if he tries to run."

"Well, that helps! Helps lots! Thank you. But that's another problem. When I see him, how *do* I sound the alarm? How do I bring your men running without alerting him too? If he grabs a hostage—"

Sherwin tossed something. It was a clumsy throw, perhaps deliberately, but Stalwart's hand flashed out and snatched it from the air—a roughly carved piece of wood, about the length of a finger.

"A whistle?" He put it to his lips and blew, but nothing happened.

A noise in the yard caught his attention, but it was not late arrivals riding, just barking dogs upsetting a couple of horses, which were giving their grooms trouble. He turned back to Sherwin and saw teeth grinning in the black jungle.

"You did that, Pimple! Yes, it looks like a whistle. I made that when I was a lot younger than you are. Every boy whittles a whistle or two when he's naught better to do. Well, most of mine worked right, but that one . . . I must have gotten a piece of magic wood, or something, because that's a magic whistle. You can't hear it. I can't hear it. But dogs and horses can! You blow that in a yard full o' horses, boy, and they'll all at least twitch their ears. The closest ones'll jump. All the stable dogs'll start barking."

The second cloud had gone. "And the killer won't know what's happening! Thank you, Sheriff!" Suddenly Stalwart's quest looked possible again. "Thank you *very* much!"

"I want that whistle back, mind! Any more problems?"

"No, I don't think so. You give your men their orders, please? Introduce me as the witness who knows what he looks like, that's all, and I'll describe him."

The fat man regarded him curiously for a moment, chinking coins in his hand. "He knows you, too?"

"Yes, but he won't be looking for me the way

I'll be looking for him."

Again the dark eyes measured. "Where're you going to be? How're you going to make sure you see this villain of yours before he sees you?"

Stalwart swallowed more pride—all of it, every last bit. "You just hired a new yard boy, Master Sherwin."

"Go on, son," the fat man said softly.

Wart explained the conclusion he had so reluctantly reached. "I could be a groom. I know horses. Horses like me. But if a boy keeps walking a horse around all the time, people may notice. No one sees the boys with the barrows or wonders what they're doing."

"You're a *Blade,* you say? You bring warrants from the Lord *Chancellor?* And you're going to shovel *dung* in my stable yard?"

Stalwart nodded miserably. "I shoveled plenty at Ironhall."

"And here I thought you were a gentleman!"

"I have friends to avenge, Sheriff. This is the only way I can be sure of getting near him to mark him for you and your men. And he may not be too dangerous by then. When I blow this magic whistle of yours, I want you to arrest the man who's just had a shovelful of the stuff slammed right in his face!"

"Flames and death!" Sherwin uttered a bellow

of laughter that should have startled every horse in the county. "Good for you! I see the Chancellor did know what he was about. Me and the boys'll be happy to help you, Sir Stalwart." He leaned across the table, extending a hand as big as a cat. "Sorry if I gave offense, sir. Like to judge a man by his melting point. I didn't find yours."

"You came close, Sheriff."

Not really. Stalwart's stint as the Brat in Ironhall had lasted six whole, horrible weeks. Nothing thickened a man's skin like that did.

(12)

At the End of the Day (2)

THE BRAT ALWAYS ATE IN THE KITCHEN WITH
the servants—so Intrepid had told Emerald in
an unusual fit of accuracy. That was while he
had been showing her the dining hall, with its
famous sky of swords. Five thousand of them
dangled overhead, point down, flickering reflec-
tions of the candles, ever softly tinkling. Each
was the weapon of a former Blade.

"Sometimes the chains *break*—" In tones of
horror, Intrepid had described the resulting car-
nage. He had not been lying, just deceived by
lies others had fed him. Wart had told her about
the swords weeks ago, so she was not worried
about them. She was worried about the King's
safety, because she could not give Ironhall a
clean bill of health. Intrepid had shown her as
much of it as the Brat would ever need to know,
but not enough to satisfy Lord Roland's spy. She
had questions needing answers.

She was worried about her insight into Silvercloak's identity. Her suspicions might be wrong,

but somehow she must inform Lord Roland of them as soon as possible.

She was also worried about Servian. Servian was the worst of all possible enemies, Intrepid had told her—truthfully. Grand Master favored him because he was a good swordsman. When the previous Prime had publicly told Grand Master to dump Servian, Grand Master had expelled Prime instead. That had been Candidate Badger, of course, and Emerald knew things about Badger she was sworn never to reveal. She could certainly use him at her side right then to defend her against Servian and his cronies.

Common sense insisted she go straight to Grand Master and admit that he had been right and she could not carry off this imposture. What could it achieve? If Silvercloak really was a woman, Ironhall was absolutely the last place she would attempt to strike at the King. Alas, people as stubborn as Emerald did not always listen to common sense.

The evening meal was about to start. She lurked in the kitchen doorway, watching the entrance to the hall. The cooks were all men, mostly old. As long as she stayed out of their way, they did not seem to mind her or even notice her.

Intrepid had gone. Prime Marlon had tracked down the Brat and his guide in the hall and ordered Intrepid to run like a hare, bathe like a trout, and come back in clean clothes even faster.

"You may as well wait here," he had told Emerald. He smiled, but not unkindly. "I suggest you don't bother changing yet."

"No, sir." Wet clothes were a minor problem at the moment.

"Look at it this way, lad. In five years you'll be a deadly swordsman, probably living at court. If some drunken nobles come along and start taunting you, will you be able to control yourself? Or will you go mad and kill them?"

Was this how they rationalized sadism? "So it's a test?"

"Of course. If you can take it from these squirts, you can take it from anyone. If it goes too far, talk to Second." He did not explain how far was too far.

A bell tolled in the distance. Boys appeared as if by magic, trailing mud in through the front door and across to the hall—eager youngsters running ahead, dignified seniors strolling behind. Finally the knights came parading along the corridor with Grand Master in the lead. The infamous Doctor Skuldigger had enslaved people with loyalty spells, and Lord Roland worried that Silvercloak might do the same. Emerald was close enough to detect such evil, and she could not; nor had she done so earlier among the cooks and stablemen. It seemed the assassin had planted no accomplices in the school yet.

The kitchen staff went by her, pushing big carts. Marlon appeared again, bringing a damp-ish Intrepid and another senior—a sandy-haired, mild-seeming youth, hard to imagine as deadly with the sword he wore or even as capable of controlling the juniors.

"My name's Mountjoy," he told Emerald. "I'm Second. That means I'm kennel master." He smiled unhappily past her ear. "Un-fortunately, hazing's traditional. There's not much I can do about it. Most of it's up to you." Still he did not look her in the eye. "Blades can't be forged from brittle metal, and if you can't stand the life here, then it's best for everyone to find out at once, before we start wasting time on you, right?"

"Oh, yes, sir," Emerald said sweetly. "I'd hate that."

He did not notice the bite in her voice. "Don't worry too much. Most of it's just talk, to frighten you. They don't do half the things they threaten. Try to stay very humble and never lose your temper. That's what they want to happen. Right, Intrepid?"

Intrepid nodded impatiently.

"Time to go," Marlon said. Empty carts were coming out for more.

At the far end of the hall, Grand Master saw the latecomers appear in the doorway. Beaming, he rose and clinked a goblet for silence. "Before we begin eating . . ." That won a laugh, for the beansprouts were already looking for seconds.

A lectern was wheeled over to him. Everyone rose and stood in silence as he opened the great book of the *Litany of Heroes*. He read out brief accounts of the two Sir Intrepids who had saved their wards. One had survived, one had not. He closed the book and the audience sat down again in a shuffling of feet and creaking of benches.

As sounds of chewing resumed, Prime escorted the next Intrepid along the aisle, with Second and the new Brat following. They walked solemnly between tables full of leering sopranos, then less-crowded beansprouts' tables, with Servian conspicuous by his size and menacing stare. On they went, past the beardless and the fuzzies and a single table of seniors—only eight of those, not counting Marlon and Mountjoy. Again Emerald was alert for enchantment and found none.

The knights and masters seated on the far side of the high table watched the procession, Grand Master on his throne in the middle. When they arrived he rose again, smiling jovially.

"Who comes?"

"Grand Master, masters, honored knights"— Marlon turned sideways to include the boys in his reply—"and brother candidates in the Loyal and Ancient Order of the King's Blades, I have the honor to present Candidate . . . Intrepid!" Intrepid bowed to display the "SCUM" on his scalp and his wet half mane.

"Is he worthy, Prime?"

Prime turned full around to face the hall. "Is Intrepid worthy?"

Yes, he was. The hall roared approval. Boys cheered and chanted his name. They thumped tables. So Prime and Second lifted the new boy shoulder high and carried him the length of the hall to instal him with the sopranos, where he belonged. There he was mobbed, hugged, riotously accepted as one of the gang.

Ironhall had been doing this for centuries. If Emerald were the friendless, rejected boy she was pretending to be, he would be promising himself that if Intrepid could do it, he could— that he would earn such approval, too.

So what happened next? Why were Prime and Second running as they came back to take their seats? The hall stilled, waiting. She looked inquiringly at Grand Master, who had sat down to finish his dinner.

He chewed, swallowed, smiled. "You may go, Brat."

As she reached the seniors' table, the first crusts came curving through the air. *Roar!* Then vegetables. Then sausages. Those young demons were accurate! *Boos!* She reeled under the onslaught. There was only one door. Perforce, she began to run through the hail of missiles. Pandemonium became riot.

She made it past the fuzzies, but a beardless stuck out a foot and she pitched headlong. Cheers. Pitchers of water were tipped over her. She scrambled up and ran again. Everyone was on his feet and hurling. She was tripped again. How could a hundred boys make so much noise? She could hardly see through a mask of gravy. Then pewter beakers started coming, and they *hurt*. She doubled over, arms covering her head. A bench slid in front of her and she fell over it, landing heavily on the flagstones. *Big cheer!* The doors had been shut, of course. She wrestled one open in a final blizzard of food and tableware; she made her escape. Behind her, the booing turned to raucous laughter.

The fine new candidate had been accepted and the unspeakable Brat driven out.

Old men waiting outside with fresh supplies shook their heads at the waste of food and the mess they must clean up. One of them handed Emerald a cloth to wipe her face. "You're lucky we didn't feed them bones tonight," he mumbled.

The masters and knights left first, chatting among themselves, then the seniors, and so on down the ranks. The sopranos and beansprouts were last, but they came in a swarm like hornets. They divided into three hunting bands on a plan already agreed. One headed for the dorms, one for the bath house, and the third to search First and Main houses. That pack found the quarry limping along the corridor connecting those two buildings.

"Get him!"

"Fights tonight!"

Emerald turned and held up the brass token of inviolability. "I have to return this to Grand Master."

The only light at that point was a lantern behind them, so she saw them as anonymous dark shapes, but their eyes and teeth gleamed in the shadows.

"We can wait!"

"You cannot escape."

"Your doom is sealed."

None of them was tall enough to be Servian, but she knew now that even the small fry were dangerous—born warriors, faster than sling-shots, many of them already felons or brutalized by spirits-knew what sort of ghastly home life. They hadn't even started on her yet, but her shins were bloody, she had wrenched one knee, bruised both elbows, and her back must be all over purple. She was uniformly splattered with garbage, as if she had rolled in a midden.

She was also madder than she had ever been in her life.

She hobbled away, ignoring the mindless mob at her heels, the shuffle of its footsteps, its eager breathing. She climbed stairs and all the treads squeaked as the pack followed. She turned into a dead-end corridor and her pursuers stopped as if facing wall-to-wall snakes.

This area was off-limits except on business. Two of the three doors stayed locked, Intrepid had said, and he did not know where they led, but the third was Grand Master's study.

Emerald marched in without knocking. The

room was empty and dark, lit only by the flickers of the fire. Relieved, she leaned back against the door for a moment, struggling to calm her nerves.

Wart had brought her here through the unobtrusive door on the far side. That was how important people came unseen into Ironhall— by the so-called Royal Door in one of the corner towers. The room impressed her no more now than it had then: grim, shabby, and none too clean. One comfortable chair and an oak settle beside the fireplace, a few stools, a document chest, a table. The threadbare rug, the prints on the walls, a few ornaments . . . nothing matched anything else. Grand Master's taste was as erratic as the rest of him.

She was just lighting the last candle on the mantel when the man himself stomped in from the corridor and slammed that door behind him. He glared at her presumption.

"Well, Sister? Ready to admit defeat?"

"No. My task is far from finished."

He actually had the gall to smile! "Kindly remember in future that the Brat does not come in here without permission. I have no further need of his services this evening." He held out a hand. "The token, please. You may go."

"Don't be ridiculous." She sat down in his

favorite chair, garbage and all.

He bristled. "You cannot have it both ways, Sister! Either you dress as a respectable woman and perform your duties openly or you stay in character. If you masquerade as the Brat, you must bear his burdens."

"You'd like that, wouldn't you?" She stared at him curiously. "You said I can't do it, so you will make certain I don't. Well, the Brat is not here. If you will just take a quick look out in the tower, you will see that he is not hiding out there either, so he must have run away across the moor. A pity the snow has melted so he left no tracks. Go and tell your rat pack the bad news."

"You do not give me orders!" he said shrilly.

"No." Her voice was rock steady. She had all night. "Your orders came from the King, remember? I already told Master of Rituals you want to see him. I may need to summon others. Do you really want the hyena cubs sitting on your doorstep all night? They will, you know."

Grand Master flounced around and charged out. She heard him shouting, and then an angry sound like the baying of hounds. When he returned, his face was pale with fury.

"Be warned, Sister! I will report your insolence to His Grace the moment he arrives."

"His Grace may not be arriving." She would

humble this arrogant blusterer if it killed her.
"My preliminary inspection has revealed some
worrisome points. Unless I tender a favorable
report the King will not come."

"Nonsense!"

"No. One word from me and the Guard will
keep the King away. You know that! And
Commander Bandit may billet White Sisters on
Ironhall permanently."

Fortunately, knuckles rapped on the corridor
door just then.

"Enter!"

Emerald had her back to it and did not see
who had come. She heard a sigh.

"Sorry I'm late, Saxon. The wolves are really
howling tonight . . . new Brat to taunt—seems
they can't find him—talked to Prime . . . says
Second's keeping an eye on things . . . What
was it—"

Heading for the settle, Master of Rituals
came around the chair and saw the missing Brat.
He laughed. "By the burgomaster's belly button!
That explains it!" Misunderstanding the reason
for her presence, he squatted down on his heels
and removed his glasses to peer closely at
Emerald's battered shins. "This was when you
fell over the bench, lad?"

He was a rumpled, vague man of about forty.

That afternoon he had been lecturing bean-sprouts on the principles of enchantment. The door had been open, so she and Intrepid had paused to listen. She had been impressed by the way he held the boys' attention on a very dull topic.

He laid a cool hand on her swollen knee and frowned. He replaced his glasses to see Grand Master, who was leering at the situation. "Nothing serious enough for a healing. I can bandage—"

"Present me," she said angrily.

"Of course. Sir Lothaire . . . Sister Emerald."

"Sister?" Master of Rituals frowned. Then— "*Sister?*" He reared back in horror and fell flat on his back. His glasses flew off. "But tonight . . . you had to . . . they made you . . ."

"She insisted," the older man said sadly. "I warned her, of course, but she saw it as her duty. Her courage is truly an inspiration."

"Is it really?" she snapped. "Please get up, Sir Lothaire. I am here on His Majesty's service, you understand. I need your assistance."

He scrambled to his feet and kissed the fingers she offered. "My lady, you have only to ask! Admit . . . a surprise . . . never dreamed . . ." His face was scarlet. Gentlemen were not supposed even to *see* a lady's knees.

"Do please sit." She waved him to the settle. "Sir Saxon, show him the Chancellor's letter."

Grand Master pouted and went to the document chest.

While Master of Rituals was reading the letter through for the third time, holding it at the end of his nose, Emerald found herself struggling to stay awake. It had been a very hard day and the fire was hot. Here she was safe. Release of tension was having its effect.

Grand Master, who had been sulking on a stool, suddenly beamed and said, "And what else can we do to assist you in your inquiries, Sister? You have only to ask."

She choked back a yawn while she considered asking him to jump off a high cliff. "I need to send an urgent letter to Lord Roland."

The smile soured into suspicion. "One of the carters could take it to Blackwater and give it to the hostler there. He can find someone to take it on to Holmgarth and put it on the coach."

"Would you be so kind as to send it under your seal? I did not bring my own, naturally."

That was better—he would be able to read it and see that she was not tattling about him. He smiled, sickly sweet. "Or I might possibly persuade one of our penniless knights to take it directly to Holmgarth—even Grandon itself, if you will guarantee the costs. They welcome any chance to visit court again."

"Very kind of you. I also need a safe place to sleep. This Brat is going to be *exceedingly* good at hiding." Right here in front of his fire might be best of all.

Lothaire dropped the letter in his lap and began fumbling in pockets. "By the seven saving spirits! A remarkable document, eh, Saxon? Who's this Princess Vasar?"

He was accepting the situation much better than his superior had. But he must be clever. When Blades in the Guard were knighted and released from their binding, they might sink into poverty and vanish, or they might rise to great honors, as Sir Durendal had done. Or anything in between. Lothaire had entered the College of Conjury and become a sorcerer.

"No idea," Grand Master said. "Your glasses are on the floor by your foot."

"Oh . . . thank you . . . What did you want to see me about?"

"He didn't," Emerald said. "I did. Unless you know of anyone missing from the hall tonight, I am satisfied that no Ironhall resident has been bespelled, at least so far. But I cannot yet certify that the buildings are harmless. You keep conjurements in your laboratory, Sir Lothaire. I sensed them as I went by."

He blinked. "Enchanted bandages for first aid, until we can organize a healing. Nothing more."

"There was more."

"Oh? . . . nothing of any significance. Maybe the old books I brought from the College. . . ."

He was lying, and that was a shock. Suddenly she was not sleepy.

"You will not mind if I examine them, as my duties require? The royal suite, Grand Master? I need to see in there. Upstairs in King Everard House, in the servants'—"

"The royal suite of course! But private quarters are private." Grand Master had forgotten he was trying to be helpful. "A girl disguised as a boy prying around in men's bedrooms? Think of the potential for scandal!"

"Then the King stays away."

"You cannot wander in those places without attracting suspicion! The candidates never go into those areas! Especially the Brat."

"Tush, Saxon!" Master of Rituals said soothingly. "A White Sister need not enter a room to know if it contains magic. Right, Sister?"

"As long as the room is not too large and I am only concerned with really dangerous enchantment. I can sense that from outside the door. Tell me about the towers."

"Er, towers? Not much to tell, my lady." He removed his glasses to breathe on them. "The four on the bath house are fakes. The four on First House . . . all different. This one contains a stairwell, is all, and the turret room above is Saxon's bedroom. Right, Saxon? The Seniors' Tower is similar, but it has only one door. Nothing inside except a stair up to the turret. Nobody sane goes up *there* and I can't imagine anyone sane wanting to. Don't suppose it's been cleaned since my day. It had never been cleaned then.

"Mine . . . my tower? . . . The Bursar's office on the ground floor . . . my lab above it, and the turret's sometimes called the Observatory, for no reason. I keep junk in it. The fourth is called the Queen's Tower. Don't know why. Do you, Saxon?" He was lying again.

Grand Master said, "The ground floor room is Leader's office when the Guard's here. The room above is locked, and so is the turret room above that. They're said . . . they were the royal quarters before Main House was built."

"What's in there now?" Emerald asked.

Grand Master laughed. "I can't recall ever being in there. When I was elected I explored everywhere I could, but I could find no key to those rooms. The turret room windows are draped or shuttered. I have been meaning to break in, but I have never gotten around to it."

"There's sorcery in there."

Both men looked skeptical.

"Can't imagine how it got there." Lothaire was lying again.

"I sensed it as I went by with Intrepid," she insisted. "It's faint and I think not threatening, but I need to inspect it more closely."

"I shall have the door forced."

"Don't be hasty, Saxon," Lothaire said hastily.

"I have to find somewhere to put this Princess Vasar. Normally I'd put her in the royal suite, but it sounds as if she will be here at the same time as the King."

"Why not organize the sopranos to look for keys? They're turning the place upside down anyway hunting for the Brat. . . . I may have a bunch of 'em around—keys, I mean. In the lab somewhere? Somewhere." He was lying. She knew he was lying. He must know she knew. Whatever she had expected to find in Ironhall, it was not voluntary treason. "Sister, we cannot expose you to any more of this brutality. Saxon, I wish you'd get rid of that Servian brute . . . makes my flesh crawl. You need a refuge from the mob, my lady."

"I certainly do."

"How about the Observatory? . . . wonder if the rain's stopped?"

She needed sleep, but work must come first. "Would the middle of the night be a more private time for me to inspect some of these confidential places?"

"Not without an escort!" Lothaire said firmly. "Ghouls haunt the night hereabouts, especially when there's a new Brat around." He rose. "Come, Sister. Saxon will lend us a lantern, and I will show you some Ironhall secrets."

(13)

Secret Chamber

IT DID OCCUR TO EMERALD THAT SHE MIGHT BE crazy to go off into the night with a man she knew was lying. Yet Sir Lothaire's lies did not reek as much of death spirits as they would if he were luring her into danger. Whatever he was plotting could not be murder.

He led her out through the corner door to the stair, curving around and upward until it reached two doors. One must lead to Grand Master's bedroom. Her guide reached for the latch on the other.

"It's narrow out here, Sister. Stay close to the wall, please." He stepped out into moorland wind and a spray of mist. She followed, closing the door.

"Dark!" he said cheerfully. "Raining!" Even more unnecessary. "Wait a moment for our eyes . . . should have thought to borrow a cloak from Saxon for you."

"That's all right. Except I'm going to dribble soup all over your battlements."

He chuckled. "Keep away from the edge. The crenels are too low."

"Crenels?"

"The gaps you shoot through. The high bits you hide behind are called merlons. But even the crenels are supposed to be high enough to provide cover. These merlons are fakes—just pieces of wall. Any real archers out there could see all of you as you walked along the parapet . . . even your legs."

"And if I take a wrong step I walk right through and fall?"

"That sums it up. Stay inside the merlons."

She followed the sickly twinkle of his lantern. Once they were around the curve of the tower she no longer had its comforting stonework beside her, only lead-plated roof sloping down to ankle level. On her right was stone, slabs of masonry alternating with nothing, two stories of fresh air above the moor. She was glad that the overcast night was dark enough to hide the view.

"I take it the boys never come up here?"

"Never say 'never' in Ironhall." He spoke over his shoulder. "Seniors' Tower has no door out to the parapet, but a few maniacs have signed their names on the outside of it over the years."

Emerald shuddered. Earth people like her

were rarely good with heights. If Wart were here, he would be running along the merlons and turning cartwheels.

Lothaire himself was another air type, probably air-chance. He was inquisitive, cheerful, and disorganized. He might still be a very fine swordsman if he didn't lose his glasses. She liked him and was inclined to trust him, in spite of his lies.

Soon she detected sorcery ahead and knew they were approaching the Observatory door. The lantern moved to the right and around the tower. A lock clattered.

Sir Lothaire had spoken truly when he told her he used the Observatory turret room to store junk. It was even more cluttered than the Records Office, with piles of boxes, books, barrels, pots, decaying bags, crumbling scrolls, all stinking to her of sorcery. The enchantments were so confused that she could not hope to identify individual spells. All eight elements were involved and yet death was the least noticeable. There was nothing deadly here.

"What is all this?"

"Hoping you could tell me, Sister. I brought some things from the College when I came . . . seems every Master of Rituals for centuries must have done the same. You think one day this place will just explode?"

"Or I will. I can't possibly stay here tonight."

"Oh, well . . . of course not," he mumbled. "You see no threat to His Majesty?"

What she could see mostly was dust. Nothing had been moved in this garbage heap for years. "None."

"Ah! And would you care to inspect my lab also?"

"If you don't mind."

"No, no . . . glad to be of—" Sir Lothaire disappeared through the floor.

In fact he went down a stair, but so steep and narrow as to be almost a ladder. Following, Emerald found herself in another hodgepodge dump of sorcerous junk, no tidier than the one upstairs and—curiously—almost as dusty. The healing magic racked her with waves of nausea, and she realized that she would never be able to tolerate a major healing.

"Something wrong, Sister?" Sir Lothaire inquired anxiously. He raised his lantern so his face was a gargoyle in the darkness.

"Too much spirituality, is all. I detect nothing that should alarm the Royal Guard."

He sighed, undoubtedly with relief. "Good, good. . . . see what I came for . . . around here somewhere . . ."

A box of keys, she decided. That had been his

most resounding lie earlier.

"Ah, got it . . . have a confession to make, Sister. Prefer . . . of course—I mean, you must do your duty—if possible . . . prefer you not mention this to Grand Master. . . ."

"I am here only to defend His Majesty, Sir Lothaire. Unless you are committing treason or a major felony, I shall not—"

"Not *major*. Minor, perhaps . . . a minor theft, technically. When I came here from the College . . . brought, um, this. . . ."

It looked like an egg carved out of ice. It bore a powerful aura of motion, of rushing water, turbulent air. She had met that before somewhere. . . . Yes, on Master Nicely, the inquisitor.

"It's what the Dark Chamber calls a golden key." Even in the uncertain light, Lothaire was visibly blushing as he made this confession. "The College was trying to duplicate the enchantment. This was one of my final attempts . . . works quite well. Not as well as the originals . . ."

Emerald laughed as she saw the implication. "But quite adequate for Ironhall's ancient locks? And what does lurk in the Queen's Tower, Sir Lothaire?"

He sighed. "You'd better see for yourself. Can you remember the way from here?"

She flinched. "Can't we go along the para-pet?" The wolf pack must have abandoned the hunt by now. Why risk rousing it?

"Not unless you want to try it in the dark. The Queen's Tower is visible from the yard, and I don't like showing lights there."

"You are not coming with me?"

He seemed puzzled by her reluctance. "I'll follow in a few minutes. I have to round up some candles. Here, take my token, just in case." He produced another lantern and lit it for her. "And the lantern . . . Even if there are people still wandering around, not everyone here is a baby hyena, Sister. Seniors and knights don't stoop to bullying children."

"I turn right. Down some steps. Left, right. Up stairs. Left. Right?"

"Yes. Well done. You go first. I'll follow. If you are unlucky enough to run into the cannibals, I'll chance by and conscript you to move books for me or something. That way they won't guess we're in cahoots." He beamed encouragingly. He enjoyed finding complicated answers to simple questions.

It wasn't far. She couldn't possibly be unlucky enough to run into Servian, could she?

Nevertheless, her mouth was dry as she peeked out the lab door and ascertained that the

coast was clear, the corridor dark. Holding her
lantern high, she hurried off.

She arrived safely at the door she had passed
with Intrepid. It was still locked; the faint odor
of magic still lingered. She waited, looking back
at the stairs. And waited, in steadily rising panic.
She had thought the Master of Rituals was
being honest with her, but perhaps in all that
elemental racket she had misjudged him.

Eventually light appeared in the stairwell. It
grew brighter. Only when it reached the top
was she certain that Lothaire was the one carrying it. He beamed cheerfully at her as he
approached, but she turned her face away, not
wanting him to see how relieved she felt. He
touched the icy egg to the keyhole. The lock
clicked. They went in and closed the door.

He lit an extravagant number of candles so
she could admire.

"These windows overlook the moor, you
see . . . no one will notice. Wall hangings . . .
silk . . . artists from Gevily . . . candlesticks must
be gold—feel the weight of them!—mother-
of-pearl inlay on the spinet . . ."

The room was small but most gorgeously furnished, even by palace standards. Its tapestries

and carpets were exquisite. The furniture was long out of style and the mosaic ceiling even more so, but they were still beautiful and valuable, a lost treasure.

"This is the salon," he said. "Through that door is the tower room. That was the lady's dressing room, and her bedroom was in the turret above. Can't show you those tonight."

The suite had been shut up and forgotten for ages. The ever-curious Lothaire had found it with his magic key. But that was stolen property, so he had never told anyone about his discovery until now. He welcomed the chance to show it off and brag as if he owned it.

He had used it as if he owned it. His clutter was everywhere. The elegant escritoire was littered with scrolls and the carpet with discarded quills. The sorcery Emerald had detected came from a pile of boxes, most of which were still roped for transport. Rather than clean out his official quarters, he had moved his effects in here.

She perched carefully on a chair that looked as delicate as a spiderweb. "How could this have been forgotten?"

"After Main House was added, it wouldn't have been needed. And the key was inside! There's a key that fits the door lying right there in that drawer. All the others must have been lost. I suspect the last ruler to use it was Queen Estrith, a hundred years ago. Main House is older than that, but the gowns hanging upstairs are in the style of her time."

Estrith had been deposed and died in the Bastion. She had never come back for her gowns.

The sorcerer squirmed and added, "There are some papers dating from her reign. . . ." Which he had read, of course.

Emerald grinned at him. "But tomorrow Grand Master's going to break down the door!"

He winced. "How can we stop him?"

"Easy! Do you really have old keys lying around your lab?"

"Sister, I have old *everything* lying around there."

"Then put the key from that drawer in a bunch of others and hand it to Grand Master! I won't tell, promise!"

Master of Rituals nodded sadly, looking around his secret chamber. "After I've tidied up here. I haven't used the tower rooms at all."

"I'll help you move in the morning." She had just condemned herself to several trips along the battlements. "Are there any blankets or covers upstairs?"

"Silk sheets, down-filled quilts!"

"No bats or rats?"

"Sister!" Master of Rituals protested. "We do not have rats in Ironhall! And no bats, unless you mean some of the old knights."

Emerald sighed happily. "So tonight the Brat will sleep in the Queen's bed!"

(14)

Walk into My Parlor

NIGHT HAD FALLEN ON GREYMERE PALACE. The flunkies and minions had gone. Few candles still burned in the offices of Chancery, and most of those were above the desk of the Chancellor himself. He was already late for an important dinner; Kate would be tapping her toe. He must go—as soon as he finished skimming through the late mail, brought by courier or coach from all parts of the realm.

The big antechamber, which by day was thronged with petitioners, was empty now, lit by a single candle. The figure that walked in front of that tiny flicker moved as softly as a cat, yet Durendal looked up.

"Leader!" He stood, as he always did to honor a fellow Blade. "Come and rest your bones, brother."

Blades guarding their wards could dispense with sleep—Bandit had likely not slept since he was appointed Commander—but they needed rest sometimes. His stride lacked its usual spring, and when he sank gratefully onto the chair beside the big desk, the candlelight showed the dust of the road on his livery.

Their friendship was too deep to need empty greetings. For a moment they studied each other in silence. Duty and friendship could be awkward partners.

"I got your note," he said, "about Silvercloak being a woman. You believe it?" He had not ridden all the way in from Nocare to ask that.

"No, I don't. But I thought you should be advised. The inquisitors don't believe it either."

The Commander rubbed his dust-reddened eyes. "You asked me to let you know when Fat Man decides to go to Ironhall."

"And you rode two hours to tell me in person?"

No, he had ridden two hours to ask *why*.

Bandit shrugged. "He proposes to fly a hawk in the morning on the Meald Hills, and set off at noon. He will overnight at Bondhill and reach Ironhall before dark on the twenty-seventh, weather and chance permitting. Assuming the bindings proceed normally, he should start back on the twenty-ninth."

"The twenty-seventh will suit me very well."

Pause. "In what way, brother?" Bandit asked softly.

Durendal had chosen him to be his successor as Commander. Although he was an indifferent fencer by Blade standards, Bandit had turned out to be an excellent Leader—adored by his men and capable of handling the King as well as Ambrose could ever be handled. But he was a plodder, not a sprinter. He followed rules, not intuition. Whatever his loyalty to his friend and mentor, he alone was responsible for the King's safety. He would never bend on that.

"I am not trying to do your job for you, brother," Durendal said. "I hope you know me better than to think I would try."

Bandit smiled faintly. "I suspect you may be going to make it harder."

Kate would just have to wait. Durendal leaned back, crossed his ankles. "Easier, I hope. Do you recall when we had that meeting, the day Chef was killed? Young Stalwart—"

"Suggested that Silvercloak might strike at the King in Ironhall. We all scoffed. You told him, in so many words, that he was a silly kid."

"I wasn't that hard on him, surely!"

"But you shut the meeting down right there!" Bandit raised his bushy eyebrows. "Could it be that you'd gotten what you wanted, Brother Durendal?"

"It could." A good plodder got to the right place in the end. "I admit I am merely playing a hunch, but a good hunch is better than a sword up your nose any day. Remember your Ironhall lessons?—the worst of all errors is underestimating your opponent. If he makes a mistake, of course you take advantage of it, but you never count on him blundering. A swordsman must always expect his opponent to make the best attack available to him. This Silvercloak is notorious for striking where and when he is least expected. He is a master of disguise, so that he has even been suspected of making himself invisible. I tried putting myself in his shoes. I asked myself where I would start. And always I came up with the same answer—Ironhall. When everyone at that meeting scoffed at Stalwart's idea, that merely convinced me that my hunch was worth playing."

"And he's a show-off."

"Well, he's young."

"I mean Silvercloak!" Bandit said. "I've read the Dark Chamber reports. He takes on impossible assignments and accomplishes them in showy ways. The Duke of Doemund, for instance—climbed into his coach and was driven to town with his armed escort all around him. He arrived dead, lying inside with his throat cut. Obviously there was sorcery involved, although no one knows how, but his killer went to a lot of trouble and expense and perhaps risk to do it that way. Silvercloak is a show-off! The King of Chivial's Blades are the world's finest bodyguards, so he'll kill the King right there in Ironhall, the Blades' headquarters. . . .

"I mean he'll try."

"You're right!" Durendal was intrigued. He had missed that point, perhaps because he was not without showmanship himself, whereas Bandit had none at all. Or were the Commander's Blade instincts sensing danger? To have Bandit believing in the Ironhall theory complicated things considerably. "Well done! I'm glad you didn't mention that at the meeting."

"I hadn't worked it out then. But the next day you 'borrowed' Brother Stalwart. Might I suppose he is now back in Ironhall?"

"You would be wrong. I have four reports from him, if you want to read them." While the boy had not said exactly how he spent his days, the Chancellor kept his letters locked in a box with some fragrant herbs. "Briefly, I have posted him on the western road. Look for him on the way and see if you spot him. I doubt that you will, but he will see you. If Silvercloak heads to Ironhall, good as he is, then my bet would be that he will never arrive. As of this morning he had not been sighted. I am much impressed by our baby Blade, brother. I left the details up to him and he has set his traplines beautifully."

"He is a sharp little dagger."

The Lord Chancellor groaned. "Don't you start that! So you now agree with the nipper that Ironhall is a possible danger site?" *Curses!*

Bandit shrugged. "It takes no genius to guess that the King will go there soon. And it is the *only* place he ever goes where we do not have White Sisters on duty. They can't stand the ambient sorcery."

"That's the ancient belief, but there are White Sisters who do not find Blade binding offensive. My own wife is one of them, I'm happy to say. It so happened that I knew of a certain White Sister who had visited the place briefly, without ill effects. That is why, three days ago, Grand Master admitted a boy who bears a curious resemblance to Sister Emerald."

Bandit jerked upright and made a choking noise. "You're joking! A female *Brat*?"

"I've had two reports from her. She has so far escaped detection."

"That can't last! I shudder to think what the rat pack might—"

"So do I, brother, so do I! But Saxon and

Lothaire have protected her so far, and it is only a few more days. Already she certifies that there is no illegal sorcery in Ironhall—no bewitched inhabitants, no magic booby traps. She also says the Seniors' Tower needs dusting, but that's no surprise. Does this ease your burden, Leader?"

Bandit nodded. "Very much. Some of my men are certain to recognize her, but it won't matter then."

"Leave it up to her. If she wants to escape from Brathood, none of us will blame her. If she decides to stay under cover another day or so, then I doubt very much if anyone *will* recognize her."

"Does the King know about this?"

Durendal winced and shook his head. "He will roast me alive." If Kate didn't char him first, tonight, for keeping her waiting.

"Yes, it helps," Bandit said, mulling over the information. "It's one less worry."

Then now was a good time to extract a favor in return. "How many of the Guard will you be taking?"

Bandit frowned suspiciously. "Last time I took them all."

"That must slow you." Durendal knew only too well that a large party could never find enough remounts. Besides, the days were short now, roads bad, and there was no moonlight at the turn of the month. He noted that the Commander had not answered his question. Duty and friendship were on collision course.

"In view of the present tense situation," Bandit said deliberately, "I am tempted to send out a messenger requisitioning every remount in every posting house from Grandon to Blackwater."

"Fire and death, man! You would shut down the Great West Road!"

"Yes."

Collision. They stared at each other, each waiting for the next lunge. If Bandit carried out his threat, Silvercloak would have no means of reaching Ironhall before Ambrose left.

"You will block him or scare him away."

Bandit's eye flashed anger. "Are you suggesting, Your Excellency, that I *allow* this assassin to attack my ward in Ironhall?"

"To make such a suggestion would be treason."

"That is how I see it." Bandit's only concern was the immediate threat to the King; his nature and his binding were in agreement on that. Could he be made to see the wider possibilities? He leaned forward in his chair as if about to rise.

"What I wanted," Durendal admitted, "was to set this trap and then send half the Guard there, escorting a man who looks very much like His Grace."

The Commander smirked. "And Fat Man tore you in half?"

"To shreds." Ambrose had been adamant—to hide behind a double would make him seem a coward. It would demoralize the Guard. Durendal had rarely seen him more furious. "No, I certainly do not suggest you allow the killer to attack him, Leader! Not in Ironhall, not anywhere. But I *would* let the assassin start slithering in under the door. Then drop the portcullis on him. I do believe that this is our only chance to trap him. If you drive him away, he will simply choose another day, another place. Too much caution now merely increases the long-term danger."

Bandit's fault as a fencer was that he was too cautious. Durendal was a gambler. He weighed risks, but he was never averse to taking them when the odds seemed good. His flair had paid off for him many times over the years. Bandit certainly knew that, but could he bring himself to trust his former superior's judgment? Would his binding let him?

"So you have Stalwart watching the road. You have a White Sister in place. I approve of both those moves, my lord. I have always admired your dexterity. But to invite the killer in . . ." Bandit shivered. "I can't. . . . Convince me! What else? Have you more tricks up your sleeve?"

"I have you. I have the Royal Guard—maybe fifty or so, about what you usually take? Fifty of the world's best swordsmen alert to the danger? A White Sister to detect sorcery. Flames, brother, that should be enough!"

Bandit shook his head. "Sorry. Ironhall may not be impregnable, but it's not so pregnable that I'm going to leave the welcome mat out."

Durendal sighed. He had counted on Bandit cooperating just because he thought the whole idea ridiculous. Now he took it seriously, he would deliberately frighten the fish away from the net.

The spider had one last string to his web.

"There is also Princess Vasar of Lukirk."

Bandit said, "Who?"

(15)
Have Barrow, Will Shovel

Yard boys were the lowest. They slept in the hayloft and ate scraps from the inn dining room, and the stinking clothes on their backs were the only pay they ever saw—rags far too skimpy for this unseasonably cold Tenthmoon. All their lives they had been starved of education and intelligent conversation. They had never strayed outside Holmgarth and never would. Their ambition, if they had one, was to become stablemen one day, earning hunger wages eked out by tips from rich travelers. Yet they had no curiosity about the shiny coaches and splendid horsemen who streamed through their squalid little world.

They found Stalwart frightening because he had a sword and a lute hidden away in the loft and could make music on the lute. He washed his hands every single night and he wrote letters that went off on the morning stage. He seemed more than human.

Like them, he rose from the hay before first light, shoveled and wheeled all day, and slept like a doorstep all night. His only visible difference was that he looked better fed and he wore a whistle on a string around his neck. He also took mental note of every traveler who entered the yard. But it was not until the fifth day of his yard torment that he saw anyone interesting going by, and even then it was not Silvercloak.

His daily reports held less meat than a roast sparrow. He mentioned seeing Lady Pillow's coach returning, with a single passenger. The same day he noticed Sir Mandeville, an Ironhall knight who often carried letters from Grand Master to Leader or the King and so earned a brief stay at court. Two days later he saw Sir Etienne, another Ironhall knight. If Emerald was at Ironhall, as Stalwart suspected, she would be sending in reports, just as he was.

Two days after that, Sir Etienne and Sir Mandeville returned together. They had known Stalwart for years, fenced with him scores of times, but neither recognized the stinking urchin with the barrow who walked past them as they stood waiting for horses. That was comforting . . . sort of. . . .

They paid their respects to old Sir Tancred and gave him a private letter from Lord Roland.

Toward evening, after they had left, the letter was handed to Sheriff Sherwin, who showed it to Stalwart. The part that mattered was very brief:

Pray inform my agent that his Peachyard friend suspects the person we seek may actually be a woman.

Peachyard was Emerald's family home, of course.

"You believe that, Pimple?" the fat man asked uneasily. "Still want us to hit him—or her—with quarterstaffs?"

"He didn't look like a woman to me," Stalwart said, and fortunately could add, "but I did warn you that he might disguise himself as a woman, didn't I?"

"You did."

"So remind your men. Man or woman, if in doubt, hit to hurt. We'll apologize later."

Mandeville and Etienne had also passed on the latest news from court. Grandon, they said, was agog over a mass trial of the sorcerers who had been arrested at Brandford. Testimony from Snake and his helpers was sending gasps of horror through the capital.

Interesting! Stalwart had been in on the Brandford raid. He had not been scheduled to testify, but he knew the trial had not been due to start for several weeks yet. The only person who could have changed that date was Lord Chancellor Roland.

It might mean nothing. Or it might mean that the Old Blades were being kept in the public eye so that Silvercloak would know he need not worry about them just now. One more piece of cheese in the trap.

On the afternoon of the twenty-sixth, a wagon came rumbling in. Stalwart noted first that it held a few wooden crates but could have carried a much greater load. Having been a driver in his time, briefly, he disapproved of such wasteful loading on a long-distance haul. A short haul would not require posting. Then he realized that the man on the bench was Inquisitor Nicely—sinister, squat little snoop. Stalwart had enough respect for inquisitors' powers of observation that he did not risk going close—indeed Nicely was already peering around as if sensing unfriendly eyes on him.

Instead, Stalwart wheeled his barrow over to a corner where Norton was talking with a couple of hands. Or listening to, more likely. Earthworms were chatterboxes compared to Norton.

"The wagon driver," Stalwart said.

Norton reached out a lanky arm. It came back holding a quarterstaff. There were staffs cached all over the yard.

"No, no, he's not the one! I'd like to know which road he takes out of town, though."

Norton shrugged, nodded, replaced the staff, and walked away.

He did speak, an hour or so later. He said, "West."

Stalwart said, "Thanks."

Was Master Nicely heading for Ironhall? Not certainly but probably. It was something to put in tomorrow's report, but not something likely to surprise Lord Roland. It might mean that things were about to happen at last.

(16)

The Invisible Brat

WHEN EMERALD AWOKE, SHE NEEDED A FEW moments to realize that she was back in Queen Estrith's bed in the turret room and that first light was showing gray beyond the windows. Her breath smoked, and yet the rest of her was cozy. On her first night in Ironhall the bedroom in the Queen's Tower had been squalid lodging—cobwebbed, deep in dust, and its bed not aired for a hundred years. Since then Grand Master had opened the suite and sent the servants in to clean, light fires, and make it worthy of the mysterious Princess Vasar. Knights and masters had been trooping through in small hordes ever since to admire this rediscovered treasure. The Brat had found herself safer lodgings in the royal suite and slept in the King's bed instead.

Last night she had been cut off from that refuge by a hunting pack of sopranos, so she had returned to Queen Estrith's hospitality. Which was a reminder that she had things to do before the carnivores awoke. Although she had found no illegal sorcery, she had a duty to keep looking.

She slithered out from the warm quilts, washed her face hastily in the bucket she had brought with her, and dressed warmly. Then she went out on the battlements to give her wash water to the moor.

Only the kitchen drudges would be awake yet. She was safe—there was light enough for her to see but not enough to make her conspic-uous against the sky, no wind, and not enough frost to make the stones slippery.

She still hated heights. As a start, she made herself walk all the way around First House—past the Observatory with its stench of magic, past Grand Master's turret, and the Seniors' Tower. That one had no access to the parapet, but four names and years had been scratched in the stonework: "Despenser 95," "Eagle 119," "Aragon 282," and "Stalwart 365." In three cen-turies only four boys had found a way up. Or dared it, perhaps.

So she came back to the Queen's Tower and the task she had been putting off. The curtain wall began here, curving gently across to the bath house, with its bizarre battlements and tur-rets. The turrets showed no windows and had no access to the upper floor. She knew that because the infirmary, laundry, and linen rooms were directly below them and she had explored those thoroughly. Grand Master and Sir Lothaire insisted that the turrets were only dummies, but a conscientious White Sister always looked for herself.

Frightened her nerve would fail completely if she dallied longer, she set her teeth and walked out along the top of the curtain wall. The semi-darkness helped a little, but she must hurry before the light grew any brighter. It would need only one boy glancing out a window in West House and the sopranos would have a much better idea of where the Brat disappeared to at night.

The curtain wall parapet was *much* scarier than the walkway around First House. Instead of a sloping roof on her left, she had only a long drop to the paved quadrangle. On her right the fake merlons gave her a slight sense of security, but the drop on that side was much farther, down into the hollow they called the Quarry. Perhaps the low cliff she had seen from the coach had always been there and the builders had set their pretend castle along the brink for effect. Or perhaps they had quarried right up to the base of the wall. If she fell into the court-yard, she might just possibly escape with broken bones. Anyone falling through a crenel into that rocky pit would have no hope at all.

She stared straight ahead, trailing one hand along each merlon as long as possible, reaching out for the next as she crossed the gap. Her heart wasn't really in her mouth—it just felt that way. If she stopped she would freeze to the spot.

She lived. Knees shaky, head a little giddy, she came to the bath house. There was nowhere else to go. The battlements there were even more fraudulent than those on First House, with the fake merlons set directly against the gutters. There was no walkway behind them and none around the towers, either. She was close enough to the nearest turret to know that it contained no sorcery. Wart might be able to scramble over the roof to the others, but she was not Wart.

Relieved, she turned around and stalked back along the catwalk. Now she could honestly report that she had inspected every corner of Ironhall she had been able to reach.

The residents were divided on the subject of the current Brat, who had achieved something no other Brat had ever come close to. For four days now he had evaded the juniors' rat pack. He had been hassled a few times, but never seriously—never dunked in horse troughs, battered in fistfights, shaved bald, painted green, or made to turn somersaults until he was too giddy to stand. The majority view was the lad deserved credit for quick wits. The contrary opinion—which was held by all the sopranos and many others, including some of the old knights—was that those experiences were salutary and character building and the Brat was a sneaky coward for not submitting to tradition.

This Brat had unique advantages, of course. She carried tokens from both Grand Master and Master of Rituals, so when cornered she could always claim to be on business. More important, she also possessed a magic key. She did not enjoy carrying it around, because it made her feel as if she were in the middle of a tornado, but it would open any of the numerous locked doors in the school. This made vanishing fairly easy.

She did not escape completely. Crossing the courtyard at sunup, heading for the kitchens, Emerald heard the pitter-patter of overlarge feet behind her. A voice cried, "Brat!"

She turned to face five sopranos. As long as none of the older, meaner boys was present, she did not mind indulging them sometimes, especially in public places like this. Even Grand Master's sacred token might lose its power if it were brandished too often.

"Brat, where are you going?"

She knelt and bowed her head. "I was going in search of breakfast, O Most Mighty and Glorious Candidate Chad."

"Very well, then. You have our *pernishon* to proceed."

"Thank you for this kindness, Most Mighty and Glorious Candidate Chad."

She rose, took two steps. . . .

"Brat, where are you going?"

Turn, kneel again. "I was going in search of breakfast, O Fearsome and Terrible Candidate Constant."

"That's *Most Fearsomest!* Ten somersaults for getting my name wrong."

She was quite sure she had not, but she performed the penance anyway. She promised herself that one day there would be retribution for all those bruises along her backbone.

After she had satisfied the Sinister, Uncanny Candidate Lestrange and the Fearful, Dangerous, Ferocious Candidate Travers, it was the turn of her former guide, Intrepid, who was showing pink stubble on the bald half of his scalp. She noted uneasily that some older boys had joined the group and one of them was Servian, sneering nastily over heads.

"I was going in search of breakfast, O

Dauntless, Audacious, Presumptuous Candidate Intrepid."

"Then you must go on your hands and knees!" Intrepid said triumphantly. This suggestion was greeted with whoops of approval.

The long expanse of paving between her and Main House was gritty and cold, but it was too late to claim to be on business now. She set off. Her tormentors shouted a few insults at her, but they soon grew bored, as they always did when the Brat failed to fight back.

One said, "Come on! I'm starving!"

A deeper voice cried, "Stop!"

Emerald settled back on her heels hopefully. The newcomer was Prime Candidate Marlon.

"If you set the Brat a penance, Intrepid, then you must stay and make sure he performs it correctly. That goes for all of you who agreed with the punishment."

Groans.

Intrepid shrugged. "Awright! Brat, you can walk."

By the time Emerald was upright, the rat pack was heading for breakfast at full speed—all except Servian, who, tying a shoelace, lingering within earshot.

"Thank you, Prime," Emerald said.

Marlon smiled. "Is it true?"

"Is what true?" she asked warily.

"The story going around is that you're an illegitimate son of the King and that's why Grand Master is shielding you."

"Is he shielding me?"

"Somebody is and it must be him."

"Well, I am definitely not any relation to His Majesty."

"Son of a noble, though?"

She did not think she was anybody's son. "That's not the reason."

"Well, take care," Marlon said softly. "There are some who resent your success. If they can nab you at a good time and place, they may try some catch-up."

They both looked at Servian's retreating back.

Having established that Grand Master had no need of her services that morning, Emerald made herself useful helping Master of Archives decipher some ancient records. Her eyes were better than his and she wrote a fair hand. He was so impressed that he predicted she would be Master of Archives one day, after serving her ten years or so in the Guard. That prophecy seemed no more believable than her royal birth.

Around noon a revolting stench of magic

suddenly became evident in the record office.
Emerald dropped her quill and gabbled an apol-
ogy as she fled out the door. Tracking down
anything so repulsive was an easy task, although
a highly unpleasant one. She went outside and
saw a four-horse wagon standing below the
steps into Main House. Something horrible had
arrived in Ironhall.

The inevitable fencing lessons were under
way all over the yard, although the equally
inevitable handful of juniors had run over to
gawk at the team. Grand Master himself was
conferring with the carter, an unmistakable
squat, roly-poly man. Emerald forced herself to
walk closer and soon detected his inquisitors'
binding spell under the other magic. Fish-eyed
Master Nicely had come in person.

Would he know her? If he was here on the
King's business, then it would not matter
whether he did or not. But why, if he were, did
the crates in his wagon contain something so
loathsome and deadly? A traitor, even an
inquisitor traitor, might give himself away when
he discovered a White Sister inspecting his
behavior.

She went to stand at Grand Master's side,
shivering in the odious magic aura. She knew
that spell. Once at Oakendown she had been

shown a sample of that sorcery, or one very similar. Then it had been on a tooth as big as a man's thumb—a tooth that had been dug out of the jaw of one of the monsters that had ripped their way into Greymere Palace on the Night of Dogs.

Grand Master was in a foaming temper. He clutched a letter in both hands, kneading it as if about to rip it in half. Emerald could not make out the seal on it, but she would have bet her grandmother, if she still had one, that she would recognize it when she did.

". . . don't believe me," Nicely said, "then why not open the noble lord's letter and see for yourself?"

"I resent your insolence and insubordinate attitude." Grand Master, after all, was a Blade and must share all Blades' feelings about the Dark Chamber. He swung his scowl at Emerald like a saber. "Brat, go and tell Master of Horse that we need four men to move furniture." Then he noticed the gaping juniors and unleashed a roar that scattered them like chaff in the wind.

The Brat ran to the stable. She had abandoned her original shoes some days ago in favor of a smaller pair, looted from the wardrobe stores. No one had mentioned that her feet had shrunk. She returned in a few minutes with two stablemen and two of the younger kitchen hands. By then Grand Master was fuming in silence on the steps and Nicely had the tailgate down.

"This one and these two, if you would be so kind," he said prissily. "Will you lead the way, please, Sir Saxon?"

He still had not spared Emerald a glance, so she stuck to Grand Master's shadow as he crossed the entrance hall and headed up the great staircase to the royal suite.

"His real name is Nicely," she said quietly. "Senior Inquisitor Nicely. He has murderous sorcery in those boxes."

Her only answer was a scowl. By the time he unlocked the imposing main doors, though, Grand Master had made one of his lightning mood changes. He welcomed the inquisitor with a smarmy smile.

"This is the presence chamber, although His Grace rarely uses it as such." He gestured vaguely at the chair of state, the writing desk, and other furnishings. "That door leads to the robing room and bedchamber."

"And those have barred windows, I understand." Master Nicely prowled around, nodding his polished-ball head approvingly at the balcony and the large windows. "Yes, this will have to be the place. Ah, put it down there on the rug, men . . . gently, now!"

The four puffing porters were struggling under the first of the inquisitor's crates. It was large enough to hold two dead bodies, and the men's expressions suggested it was also heavy enough. Emerald's suspicions of what it held were enough to make spiders run up her back. And the other two boxes were almost as big.

"Brat! Go and put this in my study." Grand Master thrust the Chancellor's letter at her.

She said, "Yes, Grand Master," and departed. She had a clear impression that he did not want Inquisitor Nicely to recognize her. She suspected he already had.

Grand Master could certainly have tucked the paper in his jerkin pocket. Emerald could therefore jump to the conclusion—if she chose—that what he really wanted was for her to read the letter.

She so chose.

The seal was not the Chancellor's, as she had expected, but the writing was. The message was very terse.

Honored Grand Master:
You are charged in the King's name that you give
all necessary aid to the bearer of this missive, who
travels as Master Cabinetmaker Nicely. He brings
new furnishings for the royal suite, which need be
installed in haste, as Princess Vasar of Lukirk
follows betimes.

I have the honor to be, etc.,
Durendal, Knight

(17)

Contact

THAT DAY THE TRAFFIC IN HOLMGARTH WAS unusually heavy. The sun shone bright but gave no warmth; silver frost lingered in the shadows, and Stalwart's breath steamed as much as his barrow. All morning he trudged, paused to scoop, and then trudged on. Around and around and around. At intervals he wheeled his load over to the farm wagon. Up the ramp, tip, and run down again. All the time he must keep searching faces, studying everyone who came into the yard.

The Royal Guard rode in around noon. Suddenly the posting yard was full of blue uniforms, cat's-eye swords, and familiar laughter. Not all the Guard was there, of course, just an advance party of a dozen, about as many as the staff could handle at one time. Sir Herrick wore the officer's sash. There were senior guardsmen with him—men who had been escorting His Majesty to Ironhall for years, who had given Stalwart scores of fencing lessons there: Brock, Flint, and Fairtrue, one of the heroes of the

Night of Dogs. . . . There was Raven, who had been Prime when Stalwart was the Brat, and youngsters who had been his friends until their binding only months ago: Fury, Charente, Hector. . . .

Stalwart panicked. He turned his barrow and ran for the stalls as fast as he could zigzag between horses and people and vehicles. He was doing this for his King, and there was no shame in it, and one day soon he would be on duty in the palace with those men, dressed as they were, strutting around. Then, perhaps, this would be an amusing memory. They could all laugh at how they had failed to see the Chancellor's spy serving his King with a shovel, right under their turned-up noses. But, oh!—what if they *didn't* fail to see him? What if he were recognized now? He had foreseen the problem, of course, but the true horror of it had not dawned on him until this moment, and he could not face it. Sweat streamed down his ribs.

He hid in an empty stall, cowering in a corner behind his barrow, until his heart stopped racing, his breath stopped sobbing, his stomach almost stopped churning. But the problem did not stop. Duty did not stop. *Coward! Poltroon!* He was running away, shirking. Silvercloak might be out there right now, this very minute, a wolf hiding among the guard dogs.

He must go back. Shivering and sick with apprehension, Sir Stalwart pushed his stinking barrow out into the yard again and returned to work. He had fought with naked blades against the King's enemies and it had taken less effort than that.

Most of the blue liveries had vanished into the inn. Herrick was chatting with fat Sherwin outside the office. Stalwart pushed his barrow right past them, almost under the Sheriff's beetling belly, and neither man flicked him a glance. After that he felt better. He watched faces, being careful not to make eye contact with Blades. He did not see Silvercloak, and he was almost surprised when Herrick shouted to mount and the Guard sprang into saddles. They trotted away, leading a couple of spare mounts.

Wart could breathe again.

"Nicely done, Pimple." Sherwin grinned through his beard to show he meant no harm.

"You did notice!"

"I did. He didn't. There's more on the way, o' course."

From one trip to the next, the Guard never repeated its procedures exactly. That day the King did not appear, although he was obviously in the neighborhood somewhere. No doubt the spare mounts were for him, for he must always have the freshest, in case of emergency. Later Bandit led in a second party, and Dominic a third. They changed horses and departed, never noticing their brother Blade dueling dunghills with his trusty shovel. Wart began to feel much better. If he could fool the entire Guard, then the joke would be on them.

He hoped his name would not get twisted into something like "Stall-worker."

The rest of the Guard bypassed Holmgarth and went on to the next posting house. To have taken every usable horse would have shut down the highway for other traffic, and they had come close enough. They had taken all the King's stock and all the best of the others.

As the sun touched the rooftops, Stalwart realized that Ambrose must be almost at Starkmoor by now. The immediate crisis was over, but the real game might be about to begin. If Silvercloak intended to ply his foul trade at Ironhall, he must follow close on the King's heels. He must come tonight or tomorrow at the latest.

The yard was chaotic. Coachmen and gentlemen travelers alike were screaming at the inferior quality of the stock being offered, arguing ten times as long as usual, driving the grooms to distraction, demanding to see five times as many choices, inspecting hooves, teeth, hocks in endless detail. They all had long leagues to go and the sun was setting. The inn was full. Tempers blazed. The yard boys were being worked twice as hard as usual, with far less space to do it in. One certain way to earn a beating was to foul a gentleman's cloak in passing.

Stalwart made a necessary trip to the wagon, ran his empty barrow back down the ramp, had a near miss with a horse—

"Look out, you clumsy churl!"

He spun around in dismay, knowing the voice. Two more Blades were just dismounting, having ridden in while his back was turned.

It was Dragon, with Rufus beside him. Both in uniform. There were a hundred reasons why these two might be straggling behind the rest of the guard, and none of them mattered. Rufus had been next ahead of Stalwart in Ironhall, and Dragon next ahead of him. They had been bound the day Stalwart should have been bound. They were long-term friends. They knew him.

For an age they stared at him in disbelief, ignoring the grooms and horses and travelers milling close around. And he could do nothing but stare back, feeling his dung-spattered face burning brighter and brighter red. He needed to melt.

"Death and dirt!" Rufus said. "The lost sheep!"

"Lost rat, you mean. Looks like he sunk to about the right level."

"That's what happens to cowards who run away. Isn't it, *boy*?"

They had been friends, all three of them—once. But those days were gone. Blades could not be friends with a yard boy. They could not even admit to having been so wrong about him. He had run away rather than be Prime. Coward. Disgrace to Ironhall.

"Answer me, boy!" Rufus barked. His black beard bristled.

"You don't ..." Don't what? Don't understand? Stalwart *couldn't* explain. He wasn't allowed to, by King's orders, and who would believe him anyway? "Yes, Sir Rufus," he croaked. "I am paying the price of my own weakness."

"You'd have done better to starve on the moor." Rufus was a decent enough man, easygoing or even lazy and a solid but unimaginative fencer. It would never occur to him to ask *why* his former friend had changed so suddenly and done something so shameful.

"You smeared my cloak, boy," Dragon

growled. "That should cost some skin off your back. *Kneel when I speak to you!*"

Dragon was as large as Blades ever were. He enjoyed throwing that weight around. As a soprano, he had always been hard on the Brat, including Wart in his time. But even an Ironhall Brat had more dignity than a coward who had sunk to being a yard boy. Stalwart threw away every last shred of self-respect and fell on his knees.

"Please, my lord, forgive my clumsiness. I swear I did not notice. . . ."

Behind Dragon, the man bending to inspect a horse's feet wore a silver-gray cloak that seemed oddly familiar. He glanced up and his eyes met Stalwart's. Recognition was mutual and instantaneous—killer and carrot boy met again.

"Have him beaten if you want," Rufus said, "but have the hostler do it. We don't have time. And this trash isn't worth it."

"No, let's tell Sherwin to throw him out. I don't want to see this maggot crawling around here every time we have to come through Holmgarth."

"But then you'd have to admit to him that this dunghill was once one of ours, brother."

Neither Stalwart nor Silvercloak had been listening to that conversation. They recovered their respective wits at the same instant. The assassin sprang into the saddle and kicked in his spurs. Wart hauled the whistle out from the neck of his smock and blew as hard as he could.

Then it seemed as if every horse in the yard tried to go straight up in the sky, and several of the closer ones broke loose from their handlers. They bucked or reared. Dogs barked. Men screamed and cursed and backed into other men and horses. Hooves lashed out. Chaos.

"That one!" Wart howled. He grabbed his shovel—it was empty, unfortunately—but by then he'd lost sight of his quarry in the madhouse. "The gray cloak! Stop him!"

Rufus and Dragon were having troubles of their own avoiding flashing hooves, and they wouldn't have dirtied their hands trying to catch Stalwart anyway. He avoided them. Unfortunately, a horse swung into Dragon from behind and pitched him bodily into Stalwart's abandoned barrow. Rufus, trying to escape, slipped in something and sat down squelchily.

By the time Stalwart reached the gate, he knew he was too late. Sherwin was there, with six or seven grooms bearing quarterstaffs. They all looked glum or furious, or both.

"He's gone?" Stalwart asked.

"A whole fiery bunch have gone!" the Sheriff roared. "None of them paid. Four or five runaways with them. And we have injuries."

Norton made a speech: "Didn't see the man you wanted."

"You sure?" Stalwart shouted. Could the killer be still hiding in the yard?

Norton nodded.

"Your boss going to pay for the injuries?" the Sheriff demanded, menacing as a thundercloud. "Men and horses both?"

"Yes, I'll sign the chit. How many of you saw the men who rode out of here?"

Several had, and they all insisted that no one answering to Silvercloak's description had left the yard.

"Then we've got him! Sheriff, hunt him down!"

Stalwart stood by the gate with a band of hefties while the yard was emptied. Dragon and Rufus may have seen him there, but they rode past without looking, too mad to speak. No new customers were admitted and the inn door was closed.

By the time the hunt finished, the first stars were watching from the wintry sky. Stalwart had long since given up hope. He had failed. Despite his bragging to Lord Roland, when Silvercloak came to Holmgarth, Stalwart had let him escape. Oh, he could find excuses. If he hadn't been on his knees the assassin would never have noticed him. If the yard had not been crowded far beyond its usual capacity . . . He could find excuses, but he could never use them. He had failed. No argument.

Failed!

He was shivering in his rags when Sherwin returned with his men. "Killed a few rats, is all," he said.

"Thanks, Sheriff. Thanks to all of you. It was my fault, none of yours. From now on, though, you can shovel your own stinking dung."

They chuckled.

"Three cheers for the Pimple!" someone said, and they cheered.

They meant well, so he had to laugh with them, and that hurt worse than anything. Then the posse dispersed to attend to its other duties.

"Sheriff, do you suppose your brother could find some soap and hot water for me? I'll sleep in the hay, but I must head back to Grandon in the morning."

"Grandon?" the fat man said thoughtfully. "Grandon? You saw your killer, didn't you?"

"Yes, but now he's been frightened away he . . ."

He is still the cleverest man I have ever met.

A man like that would have guessed right away that Stalwart had been posted in Holmgarth to watch for him heading toward Ironhall. With his plot exposed, he must now back off and try again another day, yes? That was what Stalwart had assumed, but suppose Silvercloak guessed that he would guess that way—that they all would? Suppose he just went on as if nothing had happened? Did the unexpected.

Stalwart studied the sly gleam in the Sheriff's eye.

"Or perhaps not."

Sherwin chuckled. "Worth a try?"

"Yes! Quickly! Hot water and soap and the freshest horse you have left. Send a note to Durendal in the morning, will you? Tell him what happened and say I've gone to warn Sir Bandit."

But he could not hope to reach Ironhall before the killer did.

(18)

Bait in the Trap

As the sun touched the western tors, the Guard was sighted on the Blackwater road. A scurry of activity swept through Ironhall, especially through the kitchens, because young swordsmen who had spent all day in the saddle were usually capable of eating their horses. The seniors bolted to their quarters to clean up. Emerald felt a great surge of relief that her ordeal was almost over. She took the news to Grand Master, and found him in his study, poring over account books.

"About time!" he responded sourly. "Wait out there until I need you. The Brat has ritual duties to perform. He summons the seniors who are to be bound, and tomorrow night he will present the candidates with their swords during the binding itself."

"I have no objection to herding seniors for you," she said cheerfully, "but the entire Guard will not get me inside the Forge, not tomorrow nor ever."

Evidently he had not thought of that problem, for he pouted. "When we have no Brat, the most junior soprano takes over. Intrepid? Wasn't that the name he took? Well, we can inform him later."

"You wish me to continue my masquerade?" She had inspected Queen Estrith's long-abandoned gowns. Their style was so old-fashioned as to seem exotic, but they would be a reasonable fit. Parading into the hall on the King's arm was an amusing fantasy.

Grand Master attempted a smile, which never suited him. "Until I have spoken with His Grace, certainly. I assume he is aware of your presence here."

"And what of the inquisitor's presence? He is still working his foul deeds in the royal suite." She could catch whiffs of black magic even here, in First House.

"Another topic I shall discuss with His Majesty. Go."

She mockingly bobbed him a curtsey, which threw him off balance. "Be so kind, sir, as to inform Commander Bandit as soon as possible that I wish to see him." She turned her back on his outraged glare.

She settled on the bench in the corridor and prepared for a dull wait. The two doors opposite, she now knew, were of no interest, leading to pantries in which were stored dishes used only on the rare occasions when the entire Order assembled in Ironhall.

Commander Bandit came up the stairs and along the passage to her. He was dusty and muddy, but gave her his customary friendly smile. Having glanced around to make sure they were unobserved, he kissed her hand.

"I would not have known, Sister."

"That's not very complimentary, Commander."

He laughed. "I can't win, can I? If I say you are far too beautiful even to be mistaken for a boy, you would still take offense. That's also true, of course. Take your pick of insults."

"Who else knows?"

"No Blades but me. The King hasn't mentioned it. Who knows here?"

"Just Grand Master and Master of Rituals."

He shook his head in disbelief. "You are incredible, Sister! Not even a black eye! I hope the Blades will be less easily fooled—it's our job to be suspicious, you know. The password for tonight is, 'The stars are watching.' The rejoinder is, 'But they keep their secrets.' If you are challenged, that should keep you out of the dungeons."

"There aren't any dungeons!"

"There are stocks out in the courtyard. There are shackles just inside the Royal Door. And there are cellars with big, big locks."

"I'll remember the password!"

"And you give the school a clean bill of magical health?"

"I did until Nicely arrived!" she said angrily. "You do know that he's put some disgusting sorcery in the royal suite?"

"Yes. I just hope it stays there." Frowning, Bandit reached for the door handle.

"Did the Princess come?" she asked quickly.

He paused on the threshold and scrunched down his bushy brows in perplexity. "Princess Dierda? No. The King's marriage has been postponed until next spring."

"I mean Princess Vasar of Lukirk."

"Who?" Then he smiled. "She's already here."

Traditionally the King went to Grand Master by way of the Royal Door and they decided who was to be bound. The study was soundproof, so Emerald did not hear what was said.

Master Nicely came rolling along the corridor, escorted by Sir Raven and another Blade whose name she did not know. Raven remained outside and the other two went in. Briefly she heard the King booming away.

She expected Raven to join her on the bench, but he had been in the saddle all day and remained standing in front of the door. He did not glance twice at the Brat, although he had danced a gavotte with Sister Emerald less than two weeks ago.

Time passed.

Grand Master poked his head out, causing Raven to sidestep quickly. "Brat, inform Prime Candidate Marlon that I want to see him and the next five most-senior candidates in the flea room right away. Got that?"

"Total of six, sir. Yes, sir."

She collected a following even before leaving First House. It increased rapidly as she crossed the yard—lessons were over for the day but feeding time must wait upon the King's pleasure, no matter how loud the rumble of young bellies. Voices called out to her, demanding, "How many?" but she did not answer and no threats followed. This was tradition. The stars were indeed watching, as the password said, taking up their stations in the sea-dark sky. The night was already cold.

When she arrived at *Lion*, it seemed that half the school was at her back. She rapped. Mountjoy threw the door open, pulled her inside, and slammed it. Ten worried young men had been sitting around on beds. They stood as if frozen in the act of leaping to their feet.

"How many?" Marlon demanded.

"Including your honored self, Prime—six."

Marlon nodded. Four other faces broke into grins of worried relief. Five fell. Grand Master always sent for those who were to be bound plus the one who would become Prime, which in this case was Standish.

Emerald followed them as they marched off along the corridor, past the whispers and curious eyes, downstairs, across the yard to First House. Only she knew that one man was missing. The current Prime leading this parade ought to be Wart. Under the charter, he should be the next man bound. The King was not playing by the rules.

Yes, Wart had been enrolled in the Guard, but he could not go armed into the King's presence. He would never be a proper Blade until he had been bound. She wondered where he was and what he could be doing that was more important than guarding his ward, right here in Ironhall this night.

(19)

Lonesome Road

STARS SHONE GOLD ON INDIGO AS STALWART rode out of Holmgarth, following the Great West Road. Although the livery stable was out of fresh mounts, Sherwin had done him proud by loaning him a horse of his own, a chestnut mare named Yikes.

"Call her that 'cos she's a tad skittish," he explained. "A Blade can handle her. She's got stamina like you never saw. *An' I wan' her back!*"

"You shall have her back, Sheriff," Stalwart promised. "You hold the best security I can give." He meant his lute, which he loved almost as much as *Sleight*. "And I shall tell the Chancellor how helpful you have been."

So he shot out of the yard, letting his nervy horse run off her excess energy for the first league or so. He had a long way to go and no moon before dawn. But with a good mount, a dark lantern, his rapier at his side, gold in his pouch, all he needed was fair chance. Those and a lot of endurance would bring him to Ironhall before daybreak.

Failure was still a sour taste in his mouth. He had come so close! He could not even understand what he had done wrong. Silvercloak had ridden out in the stampede, obviously, but why had Norton and the other hands not seen him go? He had not been disguised when Stalwart saw him—at least he had been wearing the same face as he had in Quirk Row, which was the face the men had been told to look out for. Could even a magical disguise be changed so swiftly?

It was something to think about in the night.

The posting house at Beaslow was dark and closed. Knowing she had done her fair share, Yikes nickered hopefully. She could scent other horses and sweet hay. Normally a Blade would bang on the doors and shutters until he got service, but there was small chance of finding a better mount in Beaslow after the Guard had passed through. Moreover, Stalwart lacked a binding scar. Several times since he joined the Old Blades he had been challenged to justify his cat's-eye sword. Always he had got by with some bluster, sometimes flaunting a flashy document or his White Star. Tonight he had neither of those with him. A hostler hauled out of bed at this hour might well insist on the letter of the law.

"Sorry, Your Highness," he said. "We have a long way to go yet." He rode on by, into the dark and cold. But Yikes could not carry him all the way to Ironhall.

(20)

Princess Vasar

"BROTHERS, CANDIDATES," GRAND MASTER declaimed. "Before our customary reading from the *Litany*, I have His Grace's permission to make an important announcement."

He had been relegated to a stool, like the other masters. The King occupied the throne, overflowing it, making it look much smaller than usual. Ironhall swarmed with Blades. Some were eating at the seniors' table; others stood guard along the walls. There were even Blades in the kitchen, tasting the royal food and escorting it every step of the way to the table. Master Nicely was nowhere in sight, still tending his own vile business elsewhere.

Emerald stood in the doorway, studying the gathering. A wise Brat ate early and left early, and it was almost time for her to disappear. Hazing was officially frowned on before bindings, because the Brat ought to be left in his right mind for the ritual, but she did not trust the likes of Servian and his henchmen to observe such rules.

"It is not only His Majesty who honors us tonight but also many companions in our Order—as you may have noticed." Grand Master's attempts at humor rarely won smiles, let alone laughter. "They are welcome, but they are dangerous. If they were not dangerous, Ironhall would not have done its duty by them. In normal times we tolerate a certain amount of illegal activity in the hallways after lights-out. Recently it has been less productive than usual, I understand." That small witicism did raise some sniggers. "However, there must be none of that during our guests' stay. None whatsoever! If you go a-roaming tonight, you will be risking a lot more than a few days' stable duty. Every corridor and stair will be patrolled. The Blades see much better in the dark than you do, but they are authorized to run you through first and question you after. . . ."

Even at the far end of the hall, Emerald could tell that the King was displeased. There had been none of the usual boisterous royal laughter.

"Brat?"

She jumped halfway to the ceiling. She would have sworn any oath that no man in boots could have approached her undetected over the paving stones. She spun around angrily, and found herself nose-to-nose with Sir Fury, who was certainly not the largest of the Blades but might well be the cutest.

He said, "Sorry! Wonderful reflexes! You can be proud of those, boy. Glad you're not armed!"

Ironhall humor, no doubt. Emerald just blushed scarlet, and he fortunately misunderstood. "Leader wants to see you, lad. Come."

She had danced only one gavotte with Raven. But with young Sir Fury she had danced a multitude of gavottes—also minuets, courantes, and quadrilles—on several evenings. Sir Fury had expressed serious interest in Sister Emerald. And here he had failed to recognize her! He would never forgive her when the truth came out.

She walked beside him in silence, knowing that some people recognized voices more readily than faces. As they passed the great stair, she glanced up and saw four Blades guarding the door to the royal suite. Others were patrolling the hallways.

Halfway along the corridor to First House, she realized that Fury was stealing glances at her.

"Do you by any chance have a sister, Brat?"

"No, sir."

"Fury's my name. Cousins, then? There's a girl at court who looks very like you."

"I'm sorry for her."

Fury sighed. "Don't be. She's gorgeous!"

Emerald felt her face warming up again. "Then are you certain she looks like me, Sir Fury?"

"There's a strong resemblance. I'm desperately in love with her, and I think she likes me but can't bring herself to say so. She's very shy, you see."

Emerald probably turned purple about then, but apparently he did not notice. Shy? *She?*

The guardroom was full of Blades—snacking, dicing, talking, or sharpening swords. Some were doing several of those things at the same time. A few were changing their clothes. They took no notice as the Brat was escorted through and ushered into Leader's room, the lowermost chamber of the Queen's Tower. It was circular, of course, sparsely furnished but well cluttered with masculine junk—swords, fencing masks, boots, rope, axes, horse tack, lanterns, and document chests. Commanders came to Ironhall and were gone again in a couple of days, following their king. For centuries, none of them had found time to tidy up.

Bandit had been reading papers under a candelabra. When the door had been safely closed, he stood up and offered her a stool. He looked tired and beset, but he managed his usual smile. "Why are you grinning?"

"Because the last time I parted from Sir Fury, he was extremely eager to kiss me."

The Commander cleared his throat loudly and sat down. "Understandable, but let's not make this any more complicated than we have to. I assume you're not crazy enough to sleep in the sopranos' dorm. Where can I find you tonight if I need you?"

"*Falcon*'s empty just now. I have a key." *Falcon* was an overflow dorm for seniors.

Bandit nodded. "Tell the guards downstairs if you sense anything untoward. Did you hear Grand Master's announcement?"

"Some. I assume it was about Nicely's pets?"

"He was told not to mention them specifically, but we want as few candidates eaten as possible."

"They're the same as the monsters on the Night of Dogs?"

Bandit grimaced. "They're copies. Nicely claims these are more controllable, but I don't put much stock in that. He's going to loose two of them to roam the moor and leave the largest inside the royal suite. That suite is easily recognized, you see—it has the only balcony in the school, it has the royal coat of arms in the windows and over the door at the top of the big stair. Lord Chancellor Roland is most anxious for Silvercloak to drop in and be torn limb from limb."

"By a dog? He killed Demise and Chefney."

"Sister, we worked in *teams* on those brutes! The only man who managed to kill one single-handed was Durendal, and his was one of the smallest. Worry more over how we get out of here if Nicely can't put the horrors back to sleep and nail them up in their crates. Spirits! That thing in the suite is the size of a pony."

"So the King sleeps in the Queen's Tower?"

"State secret." Bandit's smile said she had guessed correctly.

"And Princess Vasar of Lukirk is the dog?"

"It's a code for all three dogs." He rubbed his eyes wearily. "I wish I never let Durendal talk me into this! You know, Sister, if you include the seniors and the knights, we must have close to a hundred able swordsmen in Ironhall tonight, not to mention three monsters. And there's only one man out there in the dark! So why do I feel besieged?"

He was an honest man doing his best, and she felt angry at Lord Roland for adding to his burdens. Yet the situation was not really Roland's doing. At least he had seen the danger and taken precautions.

"Could you have stopped the King coming to Ironhall?"

"Probably. But he would soon have found himself a new Leader."

"Does he know I'm the Brat?"

Bandit shrugged. "Not from me. From Roland maybe. The King knows only what the King admits to knowing, Sister. He's in a monumentally foul temper, but that may just be from finding Nicely here and having to sleep in a strange bed—and the very idea that there could be royal quarters like the Queen's Tower existing unknown in Ironhall all this time did *not* improve his mood! White Sisters and inquisitors are not things he associates with Ironhall. He doesn't want to be bothered with those here. He looks on his Ironhall excursions as recreation. He hates to think his Blades are not capable of protecting him."

"I can't be Brat at the binding."

"No, we'll let you off that. Ambrose is very sensitive to scandal, too. A woman in Ironhall sets his teeth on edge."

"Does Master Nicely know I'm here?"

"Not from me," Bandit said sharply. He might enjoy deceiving the inquisitor or perhaps did not trust him—Blades trusted no one except one another.

"I'll stay the Brat for now," she agreed. "But then you owe me a favor."

"Name it."

"You did tell one man who the Brat really is, didn't you?"

Bandit nodded sheepishly. "Had to warn him when I sent him to fetch you. Didn't want him letting any cats out of bags."

"Give me your solemn promise that you will not tell him you told me you'd told him!"

"Er . . . I promise."

Oh, did young Fury have something coming to him!

(21)
The Way into
My Parlor

NOT A DOG BARKED IN BLACKWATER. THE hamlet lay like a corpse under the stars, with only a rare bat squeak to show life. Yikes was footsore and far too weary to attempt the climb onto Starkmoor.

Stalwart thundered on the hostler's door with the hilt of his sword. "Longberry!" he yelled. "Osbert Longberry! In the King's name!"

Osbert must sleep soundly. He was not in Sherwin's class for thinking—not the fleetest steed in the meadow, Snake said—but he was painstaking and honest.

"Know you," said a growl from an upper window. "You're Sir Stalwart."

"You have wonderful eyesight!"

"Knew your voice. Gave me a silver groat, you did."

"I did. I'll give you a gold crown tonight."

Osbert cackled but stayed at the window. "In a hurry to catch up with the King, likely? Called me by name, he did. 'Good chance to you, Master Longberry,' he says. Always remembers me, His Majesty does, spirits bless 'im."

So much for Bandit's efforts at security!

"And I ride on his service. But tell me, did another man come this way tonight, after the King and the Blades?"

"Well, old Will up the valley, and farmer—"

"A stranger?"

"Oh, a stranger . . . darkish fellow, hooked nose? All alone. Very jumpy sort, peering everywhere?"

"That sounds like him," Stalwart said. "How about a horse?" Or dawn would find him frozen to death on this doorstep.

"Nothing left. Need their sleep, horses do. Came a long way."

"*Two* gold crowns?" Bribery might not work on Osbert; he loved horses much more than money.

"Well there's Lumpkin," he said reluctantly.

"What's wrong with Lumpkin?"

"Nothing. Big strong gelding. Just some folks think he's got a hard trot."

"Lumpkin will do fine. He'll keep me awake. *Now, please, Master Longberry!*"

So Yikes found her dry stall, with oats and a good rubdown to come—Osbert would not

skimp. He solemnly swore he would keep the
mare just for Stalwart, not trade her away. He
saddled up Lumpkin, who was indeed a tower
of muscle. And a very hard ride.

Stalwart paid the two crowns and set off up
the moor trail, feeling as if he were being
bounced on a picket fence.

The night was cryptically still, a huge icy
silence broken only by the steady clop of his
horse's hooves. Stars filled the sky to bursting. It
was long after midnight before he saw the black
bulk of Ironhall rise against them.

His lantern's feeble glow writhed over the
trail ahead. So far as he was aware—which was
not very far—the Guard never patrolled outside
the walls. He hoped his light would be noticed,
because to sneak up on the Royal Guard was an
excellent way of becoming very dead. Not that
he was far off dead now. Cold and a sense of
failure had sunk deep into his bones. All the
long hours of clop . . . clop . . . clop . . . Not to
mention the pounding from Lumpkin—

Panic! The gelding tossed up his head and
screamed a whinny, then jittered sideways,
catching his rider by surprise. It was the first
spark of personality he'd shown.

"Easy, fellow, easy! *Lumpkin!* Nothing to be

scared of." Stalwart wrestled him under control, although he remained skittish. "What spooked you, lad?" Then an owl soared in silence overhead and he laughed. "Never seen an owl before?"

He had decided to bypass the gate. The Royal Door would be less public. It would certainly be guarded, but the mere fact that he knew enough to go to it should allay some suspicion.

He veered off onto the almost invisible path that led around the back of Main House. Candlelight glowed in the King's windows, with the royal heraldry in them as blazon stains of red and blue. Candidates were never allowed inside the royal suite, but there was a balcony outside the presence chamber. Anywhere a squirrel could go, the younger Stalwart had gone. He had peered in those windows—had even taken a peek in the window of the next room, clinging to the bars with his feet dangling. What a crazy kid he had been!

The lights meant that there were Blades in there, standing watch outside the King's bedroom. In fact they would be sprawled on the floor, playing dice. No matter. Either Bandit or Dreadnought would be in charge. Stalwart could flip a few pebbles up at the door and introduce himself. But then he might break one of the King's windows or waken the big man himself, and His Grace could be very ungraceful when he wanted to be. Better stick to the original plan.

The tower, when he reached it, was dark. He had expected to see light in the windows beside the Royal Door. Surprisingly, there was a glow of candles visible up in Grand Master's study, so either the old sourpuss had not yet gone to bed or the Guard had taken it over.

He groaned as he slid from the saddle. Never had he been more pleased to end a journey. He tied the reins to the rail and patted the gelding's neck. "Well done, big fellow. I'll beg some oats for—"

Again Lumpkin whinnied in alarm, jerking at his tether, stamping feet. "Whoa, there!" Stalwart laughed. "Easy! You're too big to be an owl's supper."

Leaving the lantern to comfort the animal, he hobbled over to the door. There *were* chinks of light showing above and below it, so the windows had been draped. He hammered on the planks and then hopefully tried a tug on the latch string, and felt movement. A gentle push at the door made it creak open a finger width. This seemed suspicious, if not downright hair-raising.

Normally this postern was left unlocked for the use of secret visitors, but tonight it should be barred, surely?

"Friend!" he said. "Stalwart of the Royal Guard. I bring an urgent report for Commander Bandit or Sir Dreadnought."

No reply.

Thinking, *Here goes!* he put a foot against the door and pushed. It was stiffer than he expected. He pushed harder and suddenly it flew wide. He stumbled off balance.

He had been so long in the dark that even candles could dazzle him for a moment. A moment was long enough. Hands jerked him forward. He was tripped and slammed facedown on the floor. The door thundered shut behind him, a bolt thudded home.

A sword point pricked his back, right above his heart.

"One twitch and you're dead," Dragon said. An unseen hand slid *Sleight* from her scabbard and took her away.

"I recall a candidate called Stalwart," a deep voice remarked. "Didn't know he'd been bound."

"He wasn't." That was Panther. "He was next behind us three."

Rufus: "Should have been Prime—"

"—but he ran away," Dragon finished.

"Wha-a-at?" scoffed the unidentified man. "You're telling me *Prime* ran away? Nonsense! I'd have heard about that."

"He never was Prime." Panther was a decent guy, with more brains than either Dragon or Rufus. "He disappeared before we were bound. He was always lippy, so we thought he must've sassed Grand Master once too often, but the old man swore he hadn't puked him. He just puked himself."

"Di'n't wanna tell anyone this," Dragon muttered. "But we saw him today, Rufe an' me. He was shoveling horse stuffing in the posting yard at Holmgarth. Dressed in rags, stinking, an' filthy an'—"

"Isn't it about time," yelled a voice from the floor, "that somebody asked me for my side of the story? I came here with a very urgent message for Leader, and you are treating me like . . . like . . ." Like Silvercloak would be treated. "You may not believe this, *brothers,* but I'm as much a member of the Royal Guard as any one of you." They had better believe it, or he was in trouble!

"That's a genuine cat's-eye sword," said the deep voice. "Lovely rapier. Name of *Sleight.* That familiar?"

Two men grunted, meaning no.

Panther said, "Does sound like what Wart might name a sword. And he'd no use for sabers."

"Well, let him sit up. Remember what Leader said. He may not be who he looks like. At the least sign of trouble, strike."

Moving very gingerly, Stalwart rolled over and sat up. He crossed his legs. He could see two swords pointed at him and guessed that there were two more at his back. The deep voice belonged to Sir Fitzroy, one of the senior guardsmen. He would undoubtedly have been knighted and released by now had it not been for the Monster War. He wore the sash, of course. No one would trust any of those other baboons with responsibility.

Like the Seniors' Tower, this one was a hollow drum, with a spiral staircase winding up the wall, complete with marble bannister. Rusty iron shackles in the walls suggested that horses had once been kept there, or it had been used as a punishment cell. It was off-limits to candidates, but anytime Stalwart had peeked in, it had been empty. It had been empty when he came through with Emerald. Tonight some stools and candles had been added, plus a rug so the watchers could roll dice, the Blades' invariable antidote for boredom.

"You look like I remember," Fitzroy said. "Explain."

"Watch him, brother," Rufus growled. "He's nimbler than a cricket."

"I know. I remember the last time I tried him on rapiers."

Stalwart ignored that. "The day these three and Orvil were accepted for binding, Leader took me aside and offered me a special enlistment into the Guard before I was bound."

"That's nonsense."

"The King—*Fat Man!*—approved it. They needed someone to track down some sorcerers, to help Snake. Which I did. Which I have continued to do. And today I was on a special posting for Durendal. I'd have hoped that old friends might have given me the benefit of a little doubt." He glared up at Rufus. If he had the grace to blush, which he probably did not, his massive black beard hid it.

"It's illegal to wear a sword like that without a binding scar," Fitzroy said. "Show it."

"I told you, my binding was postponed! And if you think Silvercloak could disguise himself to look this much like me, wouldn't he be able to fake a little sword scar?"

"If he thought of it."

"Silver who?" Dragon said.

Fitzroy looked even less trustful now. "That's the man we're watching for, but not many people were told his name."

"Oh, this is ridiculous!" Stalwart said. "Fetch Leader! Or Dreadnought. Or Grand Master! Or Master of Archives! Any of them will vouch for me. Or the King. I've played lute duets with him, burn you!" He should guard his tongue—why not tell them about his White Star and end the conversation completely?

Fitzroy said, "You three knew Stalwart. Is this him?"

Rufus and Dragon made uncertain noises.

Panther said, "Yes. And I never did believe he'd run away. I thought Grand Master was lying."

"We'll take him upstairs. Search him."

"Up!" Rufus said, nudging the prisoner with a toe. "Should tie his hands?"

Fitzroy hesitated. Then—"No. I won't risk binding a brother Blade."

Nevertheless, they made Stalwart remove his cloak. They searched him and took away his scabbard and baldric.

Were he not so tired and discouraged, he would have been spitting fire. As it was, he fumed. "I can understand your having doubts about me, Sir Fitzroy, but these dogs will kneel when they apologize to me. Or I will make them kneel." Dueling was a serious offense in the Guard, but it happened.

Fitzroy, granted, was looking unhappy. "You know we must do our duty. Up you go. Panther, Dragon, stay here. You will not open that door if the King himself orders it, understand?"

The stair was narrow. Fitzroy went first, the prisoner second, and Rufus followed with drawn sword.

It occurred about then to Stalwart that the only other time he had come up these stairs, some two months ago, he had been less than tactful in his encounter with Grand Master. He had done his best to humiliate the old black-guard. He had succeeded very well. Chance, as they said, was a great leveler. . . .

Fitzroy knocked and pushed open the door. Grand Master and Master Inquisitor Nicely were lounging on either side of the dying fire. A chess set on the table revealed how they had spent their evening. The candles had burned down to stumps; the air reeked of tallow, wood smoke, and wine.

"Pardon the intrusion, Grand Master," Fitzroy said. "Sir Rufus, cover that other door. Gentlemen, this person claims to be a companion in the Order, although he admits he has no binding scar. He was carrying this rapier, which certainly looks authentic." He laid *Sleight* on the table. "He says you can vouch for him."

"He does, does he?" Grand Master leaned back in his chair. "He was a candidate here, certainly . . . Stalwart, I think. That right, boy? 'Stalwart' was what you called yourself?"

The glint of spite in his eyes sent Stalwart's temper flaming skyward.

"*Sir* Stalwart! You know I was admitted without binding!"

"That is forbidden under the charter."

"The King ordered it! You know that! You know I came back here later, bringing a royal warrant, wearing royal honors!"

Grand Master reached for the decanter. "More wine, Master Nicely?"

"He's lying?" Fitzroy demanded.

"It certainly is not a very *believable* story, is it? Improbable, I mean. I suppose an unorthodox enlistment would be possible if His Majesty issued a special edict, but I have never seen such a document. I don't know how the boy got hold of this sword, either." He took up *Sleight* to peer at her hilt and inscription. "It looks genuine enough." Nothing he had said was an actual lie.

"Wait!" Stalwart howled before anyone else could speak. He was almost mad enough to throw himself at the detestable old phony's throat. "Master Inquisitor Nicely! You know me and who I am! You know what I've been doing these last three months!"

The inquisitor's unreal eyes stared at him without expression. "Sir Fitzroy, I have never seen that boy in my life before."

Fitzroy's hand grabbed the scruff of Stalwart's neck. "Thank you, gentlemen. Sorry to have disturbed—"

"What are you going to do with him?" Grand Master inquired with a yawn.

"Shackle him to the wall downstairs. Even if he is a coward and turncoat, we can hardly throw him out on the moor—not tonight. And if he is the assassin we're expecting, he'll do no harm there."

Rufus was at the far side of the room. *Sleight* was back on the table with her hilt toward Stalwart. He stamped hard on Fitzroy's instep, which released the grip on his neck, grabbed up his precious rapier, and spun around. Fitzroy had his sword out already, but he was no match for Stalwart. Grand Master and Nicely and Rufus all drew and leaped forward and ended in a hopeless tangle with the table. Four or five flickering parries and *Sleight* stabbed into Fitzroy's forearm. He yelped.

"Sorry!" Stalwart shouted, slamming the door. He plunged down the stairs. Panther and Dragon heard the racket and ran to intercept him at the bottom. Sword in hand, Panther swung around the newel post to face the threat charging down, but Stalwart jumped up on the bannister and came racing down that, leaning into the curve. Before Panther could spit him, he leaped off. Dragon had just time to turn toward him and not enough to raise his sword before Stalwart's boots came down on his shoulders. He collapsed with a scream. Stalwart's bounce took him almost to the door; he swung around to fend off Panther's attack. He wished it were Rufus, not the only one of the three who had believed his story.

He had always respected Panther's fencing, but that was before Chef and Demise had made him over. No time for subtlety. Rufus and Fitzroy were hurtling down the stair to help. Panther cried out as *Sleight* ripped his ear.

Stalwart slid the bolt and pulled the door.

"Sorry!" he said again, vanishing out into the dark.

Rats, of Various Sorts

EMERALD WAKENED VIOLENTLY, DREAMING SHE was choking, buried alive. She sat up, bewildered and gasping for air. She was in *Falcon*, the dormitory. It was large and dark, smelling stale and chill, unused. A froth of stars shone through the windows opposite, and starlight glimmered spookily on beds arrayed along both walls. A tiny chink of light showed from the dark lantern she had set on the chair beside her bed, left lit in case of emergency.

Sorcery! That was what had disturbed her. Earth elementals . . . death elementals . . . close. Very close! Not Silvercloak's personal sorcery but something else—earthy, dark, detestable. There was fire in it, too, which seemed wrong. It was over . . . there? . . . no, more that way. . . . *There!*

It came from those eyes . . . two tiny eyes peering in a window. . . . She slapped open the lantern shutter. The room blazed impossibly bright after the dark, and the eyes vanished. They had not been peering in at her. They were inside the dorm. A rat leaped from sill to bed, from bed to floor, and streaked along the room in a skitter of tiny claws. It vanished under the door.

Ugh! Nasty, filthy vermin! But *sorcerous* vermin? The stink of enchantment had gone when it did. Master of Rituals claimed that there were no rats in Ironhall. Death and earth would certainly be right for rats, but why *fire*? Incendiary rats? Fire included heat, light, vision. . . . Spying? Could a sorcerer send rats, real or conjured, to spy for him?

Hunt down the King, perhaps?

Emerald threw off the covers and leaped out of bed.

In the few moments it took her to dress, she almost lost her nerve. She would be challenged by armed guards, hair-trigger-ready to strike at imagined assassins. Even when she reached Bandit, would he believe her? Silly, flighty girls see rats and imagine sorcery all the time, of course. This was *not* imaginary! There had been a vile little sorcery right here in the room with her. Her duty was clear.

Ironhall was under attack! No time to waste.

She paused at the door to take stock: warm cloak, lantern, and Sir Lothaire's magic key—

which she preferred to carry, when she must carry it, dangling in the toe of a sock. She slipped out the door as quietly as squeaky hinges would allow.

Her feet made little hushing noises on the boards as she hurried along the corridor, then downstairs, lantern light dancing ahead of her, shadows leaping away in panic. Under her breath she kept repeating the password, *The stars are watching.* The hallway was dark, with no signs of Blades. Of course most of the Guard would be staying close to the King, in First House. There would be only a few patrolling the whole complex of West and King Everard houses.

Right or left?

"At last!" A man stepped out of the shadows to her left. She whipped the beam of her lantern around. A scream died as her throat seemed to close up altogether.

It was Servian.

Why? What in the world was he doing here in the middle of the night? Had he been lying in wait, hoping to catch the elusive Brat? Sleeping in corners? How many nights?

"Stay away from me!" she squeaked, backing. "You heard what Grand Master said!"

He smiled, strolling after her, blowing on his hands. In the tricky light he looked enormous, a giant. "But you didn't? We have waited too long to begin your education, Brat. We have many lessons to get through tonight. Take his lantern."

Before she realized that there was someone behind her, arms reached around and snatched the lantern away. She squawked and jumped free. There were two of them——Castelaine and Wilde, of course, Servian's favorite cronies. She was trapped. Where was the Guard?

Servian chuckled and advanced purposefully. "You knocked me down in the mud, Brat. We'll start by explaining the folly of that."

She did not see the blow coming, did not even realize he intended to hit her. Blue and red fire and terrible pain exploded in her left eye. She reeled back in shock, almost fell. She had never guessed how hard a man could punch.

"Fists up, Brat!" Wilde said. "You're in a fight. The first of several. Defend yourself."

"What's he got in his hand?" asked Castelaine, who had the lantern.

Through the thundering pain came the thought that, whatever happened, she must not let these hooligans get their hands on Lothaire's magic key. She cowered away, arms up to defend her head. Servian's second punch slammed into her back, sending her sprawling headlong against a door.

Which was not properly latched. She stumbled through it, and in a flash of inspiration slammed it shut and hit the lock with the magic key. For a moment nothing happened—some of these doors had not been locked in generations. The ancient tumblers clicked.

Servian jiggled the latch and shouted angrily. Fists hammered on the wood.

"What's happening?" Intrepid squealed, sitting up. Other trebles echoed him.

"It's the Brat!" Lestrange shouted.

Ironhall was under attack, and Emerald had locked herself in *Rabbit* with sixteen sopranos.

(23)

Stalwart Comes in from the Cold

FITZROY AND HIS MEN SLAMMED THE DOOR AND slid the bolt and did not come out to look for the escaped prisoner. Stalwart felt trapped in a nightmare, like a fly in hot soup. Why had Nicely and Grand Master denied him? He had the rest of the night to wonder that, and he was not going to come up with an answer.

So here he was, shut out on a freezing night with no cloak—and no lantern. He found the ancient hitching rail snapped in two and Lumpkin gone. Spooked, pulled loose, and fled? Spooked by what? What had Fitzroy meant about not throwing Stalwart out on the moor *tonight* especially? What haunted the dark besides owls? The lantern was a battered ruin, kicked by the gelding in his struggles. He hoped it had managed to make a getaway and was not lying dead at the bottom of the Quarry by now. Or being eaten somewhere by something.

Tucking his hands under his arms, he retraced

his path around to the balcony and the lights of
the royal suite. Fitzroy would certainly send a
report to Leader about him, but he was not
inclined to wait for the results of that. He
wanted to be *inside* as soon as possible. Either
Bandit or Dreadnought would be on duty in
the royal suite. He scrabbled up some rocks and
stepped back to aim. Not at the windows themselves, but at the door.

The door was open.

Silence up there. Candles burning bright and
ghostly smoke trailing from the chimneys
above. Yet the door stood open on a freezing
night like this? It had not been open when he
went by the last time. All the little hairs on the
back of Stalwart's neck started to dance.

There was only one tree on Starkmoor, it was
said. Ages ago someone had planted a seed or
dropped an apple core under the royal balcony.
In that sheltered, sunny nook, it had prospered
enough to send up a very spindly sapling. It was
still so puny that the Guard had not gotten
around to chopping it down, although three
years ago it had been strong enough to support
Stalwart the Human Squirrel. He had grown
faster than it had, but at the moment he had no
choice.

With *Sleight* tucked through his belt, he started

up. The sapling bent. It creaked pathetically. In the darkness he fumbled, scratched his face, lost his temper, but eventually was able to grab hold of the balcony rail and haul himself over. He felt better then, although he knew that monsters could climb, too.

"Starkmoor!" he said loudly, the rallying cry of the Order. As he stepped in, he went to rap on the door, but his knuckles never reached it. Whether he first noticed the stench or the ugly sucking noises didn't matter. Something was alive in there.

Only just alive. There was blood everywhere. Furniture had been scattered askew and if the candles had been set in candlesticks instead of chandeliers, half Ironhall would be in flames by now. And the smell . . . He had heard many stories of the Night of Dogs, of how the monsters had climbed the walls, ripped out iron bars with their teeth, and of how they had to be hacked into pieces to kill them. They stank as they died.

The one on the floor was as big as a horse, and it was not quite dead. It had trashed the room in its death throes. It was still writhing, kicking, making horrible gurgling sounds as it tried to breathe. Something had ripped out its throat.

Something or someone? Silvercloak? Nothing

human, certainly. Had the killer somehow set one monster against another?

Stalwart just stared as he struggled to make sense of this. All Ironhall had been dragged into his nightmare. The hellhound could not stand. Its head was bent backward so that the huge hole in its neck seemed like a gaping mouth, yet it sensed it had company and began beating its legs faster, trying to reach him, making little progress but hurling a chair aside. Where was the Guard? Why had no one heard this struggle and come to investigate?

If Silvercloak had sent the monster against the King, then it should have been chopped up by the Blades. If the Blades had set it out as a trap for Silvercloak, then how had he managed to dispose of it so easily? That did seem more likely, though. That would explain why there were inquisitors in Ironhall and no Blades in this room. When Master Nicely had mentioned dogs, Lord Roland had squelched him as fast as he had squelched Stalwart.

Where there was one deadly booby trap, there might be more. The moor now seemed much less dangerous than the royal suite.

Stalwart gagged. "Nice doggy!" he mumbled, and rushed out to the fresh air.

He descended the tree at a cost of two fingernails, a painfully scraped shin, and three branches. Now what? He peered around at the night apprehensively. A rapier would be as useless as wet string against one of those monsters.

The need to inform Bandit that Silvercloak might be on his way had passed. The present need was to save Stalwart from whatever was haunting the moor. If the royal suite had been booby-trapped, anywhere might be booby-trapped, including the gate. He knew a way into Ironhall that no one else did, though. As a soprano, in his Human Squirrel days, he had climbed to the fake battlements and hung a suitable memento up there for everyone to see. Grand Master had given him two weeks' stable duties for that.

At the far side of the Quarry, where the curtain wall met the bath house, there was a narrow gap between the wall and the curve of the corner tower. He had worked his way up that crevice, feet against one side, back against the other. He was older and larger now. He was cold and weary. It was dark, and frost might make the stonework slippery.

But he was very highly motivated.

He stumbled off through the night, waving

his rapier before him like a blind man's cane. Every footfall sounded like a drumbeat. He fought a temptation to walk backward, watching for glowing eyes following him. The monsters might just as easily be waiting up ahead anyway.

He must go more carefully now, for there was no path. Ahead lay the Quarry, which was close to impassable even in daylight. He should be safe if he kept very close to the wall, although he would have to fight through thorn bushes and climb over rocks. There were places where the ledge was very narrow.

He spun around, heart pounding. "Who's there?"

Silence.

Imagination? He had thought he had heard something.

He went on again, moving as fast as he could over the rough ground. He ought to be due for some *good* luck soon, surely?

(24)

The Action Heats Up

FIRE WAS AN EVER-PRESENT DANGER. NO candidates, even seniors, were allowed to have light in their rooms after lights-out, and this rule was strictly applied.

Slavish observance of rules was not what landed one in Ironhall. Out came flint and steel and tinder. Sparks flew, and in moments a dozen candle flames brightened the dorm. Behind the door, Servian had fallen silent. Either a Blade patrol had chanced along, or he was hoping the Brat would jump back into the frying pan again.

Emerald struggled to adjust to both the absurdity of the situation and the sickening throb in her face. The pack converged on her. Some, like Intrepid, were mere boys. Others were taller than she—notably Tremayne, the stumblebum swordsman who shaved. Some of them seemed amazingly unaware of how cold the room was.

"Who did your eye?" Chad inquired.

"Servian. Now listen, all of you. Listen *deep*! I

am not the Brat you think. Get dressed, all of you. I need your help. There's—"

"There's no help here!" Jacques shouted, raising a laugh.

"Quiet!" she barked. "You get dressed. And you, Conradin. You're indecent. You want to know why Grand Master has been shielding me?"

"He's not here now!"

"Catch-up time!"

"I'm not a boy. I'm a woman." She gave the stunned silence no chance to erupt in hilarity and disbelief. "Not only that, I am a White Sister. My name is Emerald, and I was sent here by Durendal himself, Lord Roland, because there is sorcery. . . ."

There was sorcery! Again she detected the reek of earth and death. The rat had followed her, or there were more of them around. It was behind her, in the corridor. It hurried by and was gone, but the brief contact made her hesitate and broke her tenuous control over the mob. Voices erupted in raucous and predictable demands that she prove her claim. She had no intention of doing so in the way they suggested.

She shouted them down. She could shout louder than they could because they did not want Blades or anyone else coming to investigate a riot. "Listen and I'll prove it. Constant!

Why were you put here, in Ironhall? What did you do?"

He scowled. "Stole a horse."

"That's true. Conradin! Why were you put here?"

"My mom died. No one wanted me."

"You're lying. I'm a White Sister and I can tell when people lie to me. Tremayne?"

"Stepfather," Tremayne growled in a voice very far from soprano. "He hit my mom and I larruped him with a spade."

"Good for you! That's true. Chad?"

True, false, false, true . . . The trivial party trick caught their attention and won their belief. Even before she had asked all of them, the sorcery was back. "There!" she shouted. "Under that bed! There's a rat!"

Chaos. She was certain that beds would burst into flames as boys with candles went after the rat. The tumult ended with one dead rat and two boys sucking rat bites. They were all convinced now.

"Get dressed! There's sorcery around. Sorcerers are attacking the King, and I have to report to Commander Bandit."

"But Grand Master said—" Jacques began.

"I'll handle Grand Master. And don't worry about the Blades—I know the password. But that idiot Servian is out there, and I need your protection. I need an escort. Hurry! I must report to Sir Bandit. The King will thank you, I promise you."

Her eye was so swollen that she could barely see out of it, but she could ignore the pain now. By the time she had turned her back to hide her magic key and then managed to unlock the door—for a few horrible moments she thought it was not going to work—her army was ready. She led it out into the corridor.

Servian and his henchmen had disappeared, but another dozen sopranos and beansprouts had emerged to find out what all the noise was about. With much yelling of explanations, the tide rolled along the hallway, gathering strength. Someone began beating the fire gong. Beardless and fuzzies came running down the stair in varying shades of undress.

At the outer door—now that they were not needed—were Blades: Sir Raven, Sir Dorret, and another man she did not know. They stared in disbelief at the approaching riot. Dorret wore the sash.

"The stars are watching!" she told him.

He peered at her face. "What happened to your— *what* did you say?"

"The password, you idiot. You want the

rejoinder, too? 'But they keep their secrets.' I am Sister Emerald and I must see Commander Bandit immediately."

"You can't go out there, lad, er, miss, I mean Sister. Fire and death! *What is going on?*"

"Sorcery. Ironhall is under attack. And I must go out there. Have the inquisitor's dogs climbed over the gate? If they have, you must deal with them for me. *Open that door,* guardsman!"

"This Brat shows promise," said an anonymous voice from the mob.

If Master Nicely's dogs had escaped whatever control he was using on them, a messenger trying to cross the courtyard might never arrive. The Blades could not just open the door and let Emerald go alone. With the King's safety invoked, their bindings overruled any lesser duty to guard dormitories, so they all went with her. So did her army, some of them barefoot and half naked. They raced over the frozen paving under the icy stars, and no monsters came ravening out of the dark.

Fists hammered on the doors of First House. A spy hole was opened, password demanded, and given. Deputy Commander Dreadnought himself admitted the visitors and was almost bowled over by the shivering tide that poured in after them.

Fortunately Fury was there in the confusion. He shied like a horse when Emerald came into the light.

"Who did that to your eye?"

"Tell you later. Bandit, quickly!"

"This way." He grabbed her arm and pulled her free of the mob. Satisfied that a dead rat was being waved under Dreadnought's nose while at least a dozen voices shouted explanations at him, Emerald ran upstairs with Fury.

There had to be more cloak-and-dagger word passing before they were admitted to the queen's quarters. Then Fury went straight across to the inner door and tapped softly.

The exquisite little salon seemed a very odd place to find half a dozen swordsmen. The reek of their binding spell would have made Emerald's head spin had it not been spinning so hard already. There was other, more sinister sorcery present as well.

The Blades' attitude annoyed her. They clustered around her, glowering suspiciously and fingering sword hilts. She knew only one of them by name, and obviously none of them recognized her. She was not your average White Sister, floating like a swan through the court, simpering at gentlemen's flattery.

"Why, Sir Fairtrue!" she trilled, offering fingers to be kissed. "How delightful to meet you here! Won't you present your friends?"

Her fun was spoiled right away by Bandit, who came striding out from the dressing room with Fury at his heels.

"Rats," she said. "Enchanted rats. They're in West House and they're here, too. Not pure conjurations, because the sopranos killed one, so real rats bespelled somehow. I think they may be spies. They're hunting for the King."

Bandit pulled a face. "I was hoping we'd got our man. Someone triggered our trap in the royal suite. I'm told it sounded like quite a fight. We haven't investigated yet."

"Proceed on the assumption that Silvercloak won." Suddenly she felt very tired. The assassin seemed to be bypassing Ambrose's defenses with terrifying ease.

"Certainly. So he's using *rats* to find His Majesty?"

"They've found him. They're here, very close—several of them, I think. And they may do more than just spy. Rats can climb walls or carry small objects. I'm afraid they could be used to ferry magic around."

Eight Blades exchanged grim glances. Swords were not the best weapon against rats. Slingshots or terriers were what they needed now.

"You think Silvercloak could send a . . . a poi-
soned rat against the King without even coming
into Ironhall himself?"

"I don't know. Assume the worst."

The Commander squared his shoulders. "I'm
going to wake Fat Man. Sir Fairtrue, inform Sir
Dreadnought. I want Master Nicely and Master
of Rituals here immediately. Sister, I'll need you
to sniff out . . . inspect the turret room. Come
with me, please."

He headed back to the dressing room.

"Just a moment." Bandit hurried up the
cramped little stair. Sounds of royal snoring
overhead suddenly ended.

Emerald waited. The magical stench of rat
was stronger in the tower, away from the
Blades. She fancied she could even smell real
rat, a whiff of sewers, and hear furtive rustling
in the shadows. A massive book lay open beside
the candelabra and the chair where Bandit had
been keeping vigil outside the King's door. To
take her mind off the rats, she wandered across
and snooped. It was a treatise on common law.
Everyone to his own taste.

He came down again. "Give him a minute."

She nodded. How did one fight magical rats?

Oakendown had never mentioned such things, but Silvercloak seemed to have a million personal tricks up his sleeve. The Sisters could detect sorcery, but rarely was there any defense against it.

"I have had more bad news," Bandit said grimly. "You want to hear it or wait until we know for sure?"

"Can this night get any worse?"

"A lot worse."

"Tell me."

"Wart. Seems he came to the Royal Door. He was unable to convince my men that he was genuine. They tried to chain him up. He ran off into the moor."

The night could certainly get colder. *Wart!* She shivered convulsively. "But Nicely's dogs . . . What do you mean, 'unable to convince your men'? He had his cat's-eye sword with him? They know him!"

"Perhaps he wasn't genuine. He was one disarmed prisoner against four Blades, one knight, and an inquisitor, but he wounded two Blades slightly, broke both Sir Dragon's collarbones so he'll need a healing, and then escaped. Doesn't that sound like sorcery?"

"It sounds like Wart."

"Perhaps it does," Bandit admitted with a

wan smile. "I'm not sure where he's been these last few days, but he certainly wasn't supposed to come here. I'll investigate properly in the morning. It may have been another Silvercloak trick."

"I hope so!" she said furiously. "It had better be!" *Wart, Wart, driven out on the moor to be hunted down by monsters?*

"Follow, please." Bandit went back up the ladder to the bedchamber.

Queen Estrith, if she had designed the room, had been very fond of frilly lace and silver ribbons. The window drapes, bed curtains, and upholstery all featured faded pink rosebuds. This decor did not suit the awesome presence of King Ambrose, who was sitting on the edge of the bed glaring, still not fully awake and clearly in a mood to chop off heads at random. He wore a woolen nightcap pulled down over his ears and a white linen nightgown that would have made a substantial tent. To prepare for his visitor he had swathed himself in a voluminous velvet cloak of royal blue and stuffed his feet in boat-sized slippers.

"Sister Emerald!" he growled.

Emerald bowed.

"What happened to your eye?"

"Naught of moment, sire. They're here," she told Bandit. "There's sorcery in this room, sire.

Black magic. It's carried by rats."

Even Ambrose's harshest critics—he did not lack critics—never accused him of cowardice. The cunning, piggy eyes narrowed a little. Extra chins bulged out behind his fringe of beard. The fat lips pouted. But he did not flinch at this dread news.

"It would seem, Sister Emerald, that we are once again placed in your debt in dramatic circumstances. Pray take thought to what reward we may bestow on you and do not skimp in your request. We shall discuss this later."

He seemed to have no doubt that there would be a later. "Well, Commander? The Lord Chancellor's strategy has successfully drawn the wolf to the fold. What do you propose now?"

Bandit's voice was much harsher than usual. "Sire, I am going to strip this room down to bare walls and put a dozen swords around you until the emergency is passed. By your leave—" He spun around and ran down the stair, shouting.

"Let us begin!" the King said, heaving himself upright. "I cannot stand this impsy-wimpsy furniture. Open that door, Sister. I intend to enjoy this."

Emerald hastened to obey, and then had to back out to make way for a rosewood commode

wrapped in the King's great arms. He went to
the battlements and let go. Sounds of demoli-
tion came a long moment later. As an antique
that piece had been worth a fortune.
Fortunately he had dropped it on the moor
side, not into the courtyard where it might have
brained someone.

"Good riddance!" the big man huffed. "Want
to try a chair or two, Sister? I think I'll enjoy the
loveseat next. Hideous thing! Should be good
for—"

The turret room exploded. Caught on the
threshold, Ambrose recoiled from the blast of
heat, throwing up his arms to shield his face.
Flames and smoke poured out the windows and
door, and up into the sky. Emerald was out of
the direct line of fire, but the accompanying
wave of sorcery was stunning. She screamed and
stepped back. She might well have fallen to her
death had the King's meaty paw not grabbed
her wrist.

He tried to go around the tower toward the
Observatory, but flames blasting from the window blocked the walkway.

"I think we shall proceed in this direction,"
he growled, doing so and towing her behind
him. He marched out onto the curtain wall.

She looked back in dismay. The whole tower

had become an inferno, sending flames leaping high into the night. Golden light illuminated all of Ironhall and a billowing cloud overhead; even the snowy tors in the distance glowed amber. The Queen's Tower must collapse very shortly and the rest of First House would follow. Without the King's childish decision to trash furniture, both he and Emerald would be mere cinders by now.

Was that true? There was more to that sorcery than just an incendiary spell.

Ambrose had a very complex personality, but the experts at Oakendown were satisfied that his dominant elements were earth and chance. "A human landslide," they called him. Like Emerald, therefore, he must dislike heights, but he showed no signs of nervousness as he plodded purposefully along that narrow catwalk toward the bath house. It was a tight fit—his right elbow brushed the merlons and his left overhung the drop to the courtyard.

They were far enough from the tower now that distance had weakened the maddening scream of magic in her head. "Sire, stop! Your Grace, there is no way out at that end!"

The King halted and turned to scowl at her. He seemed to have taken no damage from the explosion, although she had seen him bathed in flame in the doorway. "You are sure?"

"Yes, sire. The turrets are dummies. There is no walkway behind the merlons." The idea of Ambrose running up and down pitched roofs like a cat was not tenable. It hashed the mind.

"That fire is behaving oddly," he rumbled, staring past her at the inferno. "It is not making as much noise as it should. Why has that turret not collapsed yet?"

"Because the fire is not real. It's illusion!"

"It felt real."

"But it isn't."

"So we walked into a trap? Our opponent maneuvered us into doing exactly what he wanted?"

She did not need to answer. A man strolled casually out through the wall of flames and proceeded along the top of the curtain wall towards them. He carried a sword, flicking it up and down as if to limber his wrist. Firelight glinted on his silvery cloak.

(25)

Rampage on the Ramparts

"IF THAT FIRE IS SORCEROUS," KING AMBROSE muttered, "then the Blades' bindings will resist it. We must play for time until they find a way through. Meanwhile, there is no need for suicidal heroics." Backing into a crenel, he grasped Emerald's arm and effortlessly moved her past him, then emerged between her and the assassin. She did not resist, for he was right—she would do no good being a human shield. Besides, even cats would not try wrestling on this catwalk.

Although she was trying not to look down, she knew that the courtyard was full of spectators, with more spilling out of every doorway. Horrified faces were staring up at the spectacle so brightly lit by the inferno.

"Good evening, King!" the assassin called cheerfully. He was still sauntering slowly toward them, as if he were enjoying himself too much to hurry. "Or morning in exactitude. Chilly for the time of year, I comprehend."

"Commander Bandit warned me you were a

show-off." Ambrose was quietly backing away, keeping the distance between them constant and forcing Emerald to retreat toward the bath house.

"The wise physician trumpets his cures and buries his mistakes in silence. I bury my successes, but not without public demonstration."

"Then you did not arrange this meeting for the purpose of negotiation?"

"Whatever to negotiate?" Silvercloak conveyed surprise, although his face was shadowed and indistinct against the fire.

"Release of your fellow conspirators, perhaps?"

He laughed. His voice was high-pitched for a man, yet Emerald had trouble imagining any woman displaying that sort of uncaring homicidal arrogance. Although he had no accent, he used an odd choice of words, which was typical of persons who had been conjured to speak a foreign tongue.

"After your inquisitors have completed with them? What purpose are they for, then? Likewise, they were unvalued to me anyway. They paid. I kill. I collect."

Something bounced off his cloak. He ignored it. Men and boys in the courtyard were throwing things at him—books, pots, bottles, tools—

with no apparent effect except a few yells of pain from below, as the debris bounced back on the crowd. Younger boys were racing back and forth to the buildings, fetching ammunition. Pliers struck a merlon and clattered down on the walkway, joining a candlestick and a hairbrush. Unfortunately Ironhall taught no courses in archery.

"You must survive to collect," the King growled, continuing to ease back. "You really think you can get away from here alive?"

"Oh, yes! Did you ever appraise I could get in?"

"No. I'm very impressed. Shall we talk about a king's ransom? Would you like to be my Grand Inquisitor? A peerage, plus ten times what the Skuldigger gang paid you."

Silvercloak chuckled and shook his head. "I must contemplate my professional reputation. An honest crook stays bought. Kings rarely do."

Ambrose stopped moving and folded his arms. He had reached roughly the middle of the curtain wall and seemingly decided to retreat no farther. "I compliment you on your ethics. You will allow my companion to leave in peace, though?"

"Alas! My condolences to the boy, but he may seek to interfere with my departure."

"But this is no boy—"

"Excuse me," said a voice near Emerald's ankle. "Move the King back a pace or two, will you?"

She did not quite leap to her death in shock, but obviously the stress had driven her insane. That could not really be that familiar face down there peering up at her.

"Of course," she mumbled, and poked a well-upholstered royal loin. "Move back three steps, sire. Right away."

Ambrose did not stop lecturing the assassin on the moral depravity of killing innocent women, but he did resume his deliberate backing up. As soon as he had cleared the crenel, Wart scrambled up on the catwalk, rose to his feet facing Silvercloak, and drew his rapier.

The spectators' cheers echoed off the buildings and from the distant hills. From knights to sopranos, they screamed with joy. He was recognized, and shouts of "Wart! Wart!" spread through the crowd. Perhaps sharp eyes even made out the gleam of the cat's-eye on *Sleight*'s pommel.

They were seeing the King's salvation. Emerald saw a friend about to die. They did not know about Chefney and Demise. Even the great Durendal had admitted he had never fenced like Silvercloak.

Of course he could not swarm up stone walls like a human ant, either. How had Wart managed this miraculous arrival?

"Bless my celebrated eyebrows!" the assassin said. "What have we here? Last week you were a carrot boy. Yesterday you collected animal excretion. And today you're a swordsman. What are you really?"

"I'm a swordsman," Wart said. "But you aren't."

"Back," Ambrose grunted. "Must give him room." He renewed his retreat, driving Emerald behind him.

Wart said quietly, "No. Stay there for now, please."

"I manage in humble fashion." Silvercloak swished his rapier up and down a few times. He was left-handed after all, although Emerald thought he had been carrying the sword in his right hand earlier. Perhaps he was ambidextrous. He resumed his slow approach.

"No." Wart did some swishing of his own. He stepped forward two paces and halted. "You killed Chefney and Demise. They were friends of mine, so I dedicate your death to their memory." He raised his sword in a brief salute and went back to guard. "That made us all think of you as a swordsman, but we were wrong. You're not. You are only a sorcerer."

"Only? I never saw a sorcerer kneel in the dung of a stable yard."

"Nor yet a Blade. It was a regrettable expedient." Pompous talk was not Wart's style, so what was he up to? Was he playing Ambrose's game, dragging it out until the Blades could come? Even if the duel was a foregone conclusion, he could reasonably hope to delay Silvercloak a few seconds. That might be long enough to save his King if the Guard was on its way. The illusory fire in the tower was faltering, shooting green and even purple flames at times. It had stopped making any sound at all.

Silvercloak halted his approach when he was close enough to launch an attack. The barrage of missiles had stopped.

Wart had his left side to the merlons and his sword arm clear. That should be the better position on this parapet, but the advantage canceled out because Silvercloak was left-handed. Being left-handed was itself an advantage, Emerald knew. Right-handed swordsmen found few chances to practice against southpaws, while southpaws could always find right-handers.

"I worked it out on the ride here," Wart said. "It's pretty obvious now. The door in Quirk Row was the first clue, of course. And at Holmgarth I had a score of men in that yard looking for you. I had described you exactly. I gave them the signal that you were there, and some of them were watching the gate. Yet you rode right past them."

For the first time Emerald thought the assassin hesitated, as if re-appraising his opponent. "I have a very unremarkable face."

"Very. And the dog tonight—that was the clincher. You fence as a southpaw—usually. Tell you what, *messer* Argènteo," Wart said brightly, "why don't you drop that cloak of yours and we'll make an honest fight of this?"

The assassin's laugh sounded a trifle forced. "I think not. If you have gotten that far, young man, then you are smarter than you look, but you also know that your case is hopeless. Why die so young?"

"I won't die. I will avenge my friends. Come on, then, killer! Two hundred thousand ducats await if you can get past me: Stalwart of the Blades. I say you can't."

Silvercloak did not move.

This time it was Wart who laughed. He raised his voice in a shout to the audience below—and certainly no one in the Guard could play to a gallery better than he could, with his minstrel background. "Brothers! There's a horse down in the Quarry. It's in some sort of trance and there may be warding spells on it, but that's how this Blade-killer intends to escape. If you hurry—"

Silvercloak leaped and lunged, a fast appel. Wart parried without riposting. He parried the next stroke, too, not moving his feet. And the next. The swords flickered and clinked with no apparent result. Then stillness. The contestants stood frozen in place, the tips of their rapiers just touching, eyes locked.

No blood had been shed, but the spectators whooped and cheered. The experts clearly thought Wart had shown the better form. The juniors were almost hysterical with excitement.

"That the best you can do, *messer*? That wasn't how you treated Sir Demise and Sir Chefney! The fire behind you is turning a most sickly color. I think the Blades will be here soon."

When the killer made no answer, Wart raised his voice again, never taking his eyes off Silvercloak.

"Your Majesty! If I may presume, sire. There is a cord tied around the merlon behind me. It holds up a rope ladder, which this man expects to be his escape route. If you would be so gracious as to—"

Silvercloak lunged again, his rapier a blur of firelight. Steel rattled against steel.

Someone—it must have been Wart, although

it did not sound like him—screamed piercingly. It was certainly Wart who pitched headlong through the crenel and went hurtling down to the jagged rocks of the Quarry, far below.

(26)

Finale

As a skilled tumbler, he twisted around in the air. He landed on his feet with hardly more jolt than from jumping off a stool. By luck or magic, he had found a tiny patch of turf between two vicious rocky teeth.

He had guessed right.

Someone had to die after that fall. Although it was not he, the mental shock was considerable. He needed a minute to catch his breath, and several minutes before his heart stopped woodpeckering his ribs. It was easy enough for a rank amateur to spin fancy theories about the way Silvercloak's sorcery worked when all the experts in the kingdom were stumped. Gambling his life on such wild notions had been rank insanity. But it had been necessary, and it was going to change a lot of things.

The horse was still there, a few rocks over, saddled and frozen in place, waiting for a rider who now would never come. Master of Rituals might know how to de-spell it. Meanwhile, the

night was still cold and the light from the blaz-
ing tower was dwindling fast. Stalwart slid
Sleight through his belt and began picking his
way over to the rope ladder. He had some scores
to settle: Rufus, Grand Master, Nicely. . . .

As he stepped on the first rung, the fire overhead went out. Good chance and bad chance
always evened out in the end, they said. Had
that blaze in the tower started a few minutes
later than it had, he would have been past the
ladder, fighting his way toward the bath house
end of the wall. As it was, the first thing he had
seen in the sudden glare had been the horse.
Guessing why it was there, he had looked for a
ladder and found one. As he neared the top, he
had heard the King's voice.

And now, again, he heard voices. Torches
flared against the sky, silhouetting heads peering
over the edge. He did not want people trying to
climb down while he was climbing up.

"If you're looking for my body," he yelled,
"I'm bringing it as fast as I can."

"How about this one, then?" Dreadnought
asked, thrusting another jerkin at him. "I've
known ants with fatter waists."

"Lazy creatures, ants. Sit around getting fat."
It was not easy for Stalwart to try on livery

while Leader himself was toweling his hair for him. They were in the bath house. Fitzroy was kneeling at his feet, cleaning his boots; Fairtrue was polishing *Sleight*. A dozen of the most senior members of the Guard were falling all over themselves in a mad rush to make the hero presentable. They had chosen Hawkney and Charente as the nearest to Stalwart's size, and stripped them.

The King was waiting.

"What—*ouch!*—does Silvercloak really look like?" Stalwart asked as someone combed his hair.

"A bag of broken bones," Bandit said. "He dropped dead at Fat Man's feet when you disappeared. Before that—plump, swarthy, fortyish. Mustache. Nothing like you described."

"Of course not."

"I think that'll have to do until he grows up," Dreadnought said. "Here, Brother Wart, I'll loan you this." He pinned his diamond star on Stalwart's jerkin and then saluted. "Ready to go on duty, guardsman?"

It was a dream. It had to be. The King never held court in Ironhall! Yet there he was at the far end of the hall, sitting on the throne in splendor, under the glittering sky of swords. Tables and stools had been removed. A dozen blue-liveried guardsmen flanked him on either side. Everyone else was standing along the walls—knights, masters, more Blades, candidates, servants; and they were all screaming their lungs out as the hero marched in at the head of his honor guard.

Any minute now he was going to wake up.

But he might as well enjoy it while it lasted.

Ambrose was even smiling, although he notoriously resented anyone else being cheered in his presence. He lacked the crown and robes he wore on state occasions, but he did have a few fancy jeweled orders spread about his person. He was imposing enough. He would do.

And now he was rising! Kings never stood to honor anyone except ambassadors. This could *not* be real. Twenty paces . . . fifteen . . . ten . . .

"Guard, halt!" Bandit barked.

Stalwart stopped and drew *Sleight.*

"What are you doing?" roared the King. The hall cringed into mousey silence.

"Er . . . Sire, he is not bound." Even Bandit sounded disconcerted. "Tonight, after—"

"Bound? Bound? Why does he need binding?"

"Um, loyalty, sire . . . ?"

"Loyalty?" Ambrose bellowed, even louder. "The man throws himself off a cliff for me and

you question his *loyalty*? We allow Lord Roland to come armed into our presence and now we extend that same distinction to Sir Stalwart. Give the man back his sword!"

Still dreaming then, Stalwart made formal approach to the throne: three bows, kiss royal fingers. . . .

"Good!" said the King, sitting down again. "Now, Sir Stalwart, stand here at our side and tell us exactly what you did and how you knew to do it." His little amber eyes regarded Stalwart suspiciously.

The hall hushed, every ear craning to hear.

"It was his cloak, sire. I mean, the dog made it obvious. It had its throat ripped out. And the door in Quirk Row. I pushed it and instead of thumping him it thumped me, only harder. And he looked much like me. To me, I mean. He looked different to everyone . . . never threatening to anyone, because he was always familiar. He fenced southpaw. And better—I mean his silver cloak *reflected* everything, but stronger." Stalwart was not doing a good job of this explanation. "He was a hopeless fencer. I could have killed him on the first riposte—but that's what Chefney and Demise tried. I'd have died. I had to make *him* attack *me* . . . Your Grace?"

"And then kill you?"

"Er . . . yes. And he wouldn't, because he knew what would happen. So I let him drive me off the edge. He didn't mean to, I mean. . . ."

The hall buzzed.

The King frowned. "But he could kill people when he wanted to! Not all his victims died from trying to kill him, surely. So how could you know that his cloak would work for you?"

"I, er . . . I did sort of gamble on that, Your Majesty. I assumed he could switch the magic off somehow but he wouldn't dare do that when he was fencing with an expert."

"Mm?" said the King, as if he needed to think. "Stand back a moment, Sir Stalwart. When you arrived we were questioning . . . Sister Emerald?"

The dream grew stranger, for there was Em curtseying in a fantastic ball gown of green silk, all ruffles and pleats, with a long train. The effect was not improved by her magnificent multicolored shiner.

"We were about to inquire, Sister, who was responsible for that eye?"

"It was a misunderstanding, sire."

"Answer!"

Emerald jumped, sending ripples along her train. "Candidate Servian, Your Grace."

"Who?" the King said incredulously. He

scowled around to locate Grand Master. "Where is this boy?"

Grand Master shuffled forward, looking flustered. "Candidate Servian!" he shouted shrilly at the hall. "A promising fencer with sabers, Your Grace, although I have been keeping an eye on . . . Servian?"

No response.

"He is sometimes inclined to . . . *Servian!*"

Silence.

"Candidate Servian is indisposed, sire." Sir Fury advanced a pace and saluted. He had a split lip and a bruise on his cheek.

"Indisposed?" growled the King. "Show me your hands."

With obvious reluctance, Fury displayed two hands swollen and battered as if he had punched his way through the curtain wall. If Candidate Servian had done that damage by beating on them with his face, Stalwart decided, then Candidate Servian must be very indisposed indeed. Which was long overdue. A hint of a cheer rippled through the sopranos and was hastily hushed.

"You indisposed him?"

"A lesson in manners, sire." Fury tried to return the royal glare defiantly, but that was never easy.

His Majesty growled. "On what grounds, guardsman, do you take it upon yourself—"

"Because I asked him to!" Emerald said.

Fury looked surprised and then extremely pleased, in quick succession.

Emerald avoided his eye and blushed. Which was strange, because Stalwart had never thought of her as being shy.

The King said, "Umph!" suspiciously. He waved Fury away. "We shall take this matter under advisement. Meanwhile, we instructed you earlier, Sister, to consider what reward we might bestow on you for your outstanding service. Have you decided?"

"I beg leave to defer to Your Majesty's renowned generosity. Well, there is one small matter. Last night some of the candidates assisted me. If Your Grace would spare a moment to acknowledge—"

Not willingly. Normally the King ignored candidates lower than the seniors ready to be bound. Only Ironhall's finished product interested him, not the raw material. He shrugged his consent with a poor grace and scowled as the sixteen wide-eyed residents of *Rabbit* shuffled forward and lined up in awed silence to be presented.

"Candidate Tremayne," Emerald said. Tremayne

advanced a pace and bowed awkwardly.

"Candidate Conradin . . ." And so on. "And lastly, sire, Candidate Intrepid."

Intrepid stepped forward. "That means, 'without fear!' " he explained.

"Obviously," the King retorted.

The brief break had allowed him to reach a decision or two, though. "Stalwart?"

"Sire?" Wart came forward.

"We are also curious to know just how you came to be at the bottom of that ladder." Ambrose already had a fair idea, clearly. His piggy little eyes glinted wickedly. "Begin when our Lord Chancellor assigned you another of those special duties you have been performing so admirably these last few months."

Oh, royal favor was heady stuff!

And when the tale was told—

"Strange!" said His Majesty. "You mean that when you arrived at Ironhall Grand Master failed to recognize you?"

Payback time. Looking across to the far side of the throne, Stalwart admired Sir Saxon's appalled expression and the way his face was turning green, like a tree in springtime. He also sensed that the spectators were holding their breath, that everyone was waiting to hear his answer, not least of all the King. Grand Master's fate was in his hands. He wished Snake were there to advise him. He wondered what the entire Loyal and Ancient Order would say if its youngest, most junior member, trashed its Grand Master. That didn't feel like a wise move. He glanced at Emerald. Very slightly, she shook her head, which confirmed what he was thinking.

Sigh!

"Oh, no, sire. He merely declined to confirm my story. That was his duty, since he had never been officially advised of my position. I should not have expected him to do anything else."

All Ironhall released its breath.

"And Inquisitor Nicely?" asked the King, still watching the witness intently.

Saving Grand Master's hide was bad enough. No Blade should be expected to side with an inquisitor! "I confess that his denial surprised me."

"Master Nicely?" the King rumbled.

Nicely came forward and bowed, but his glassy eyes failed to register any satisfying dread. "I was merely following the Commander's instructions, sire. He informed us of Your Grace's wish that Sir Stalwart remain incognito."

Ambrose grunted and peered inquiringly at Stalwart again.

Fortunately, Wart had heard Snake tell many

tales of the King's little tricks. He was offering revenge, yes—Stalwart could exterminate Nicely if he wanted—but he was also testing his new favorite's judgment and how far he could be trusted. No one could ever succeed at court without large quantities of tact.

To have an inquisitor by the throat and not squeeze? Was there no justice? *Sigh!*

"I recall hearing Leader tell him that, sire," Stalwart said. "I accept his explanation."

The King nodded, pursing his blubbery lips. "But Sir Fitzroy, Sir Rufus, Sir Panther, and Sir Dragon—those men over there in bandages and slings? They threw you out to be eaten by monsters."

Having forgiven an inquisitor, Wart could do no less for brother Blades. "With respect, not so, sire. They could hardly accept my story after Grand Master and the inquisitor failed to support it. I was the one who decided to leave. I am sorry I hurt them."

The sopranos started a snigger, then the hall erupted in laughter and applause. Even the King smiled approval.

"I hope you will restrain that temper in future, Sir Stalwart. Our Guard is presently shorthanded and cannot afford such casualties every time you take offense."

"I will try my best, sire."

"Grand Master? If we accept his promise to behave, will you write his exploits into the *Litany*?"

"Indeed, I will, Your Grace! It will give me the utmost pleasure."

Stalwart hadn't thought of that. He gaped as the hall cheered him yet again. Few Blades ever made that honor roll, and even fewer of them lived to know it.

Then the King rose, and the hall fell silent. "Remove that star."

"Sire?" Puzzled, Stalwart unpinned Dreadnought's badge, wondering if the King could possibly know one from the other. They all looked the same to him. Then he saw Bandit and Dreadnought frantically gesturing at him. . . .

Hastily Stalwart dropped to his knees.

"We give you this one instead." Ambrose took the eight-pointed order from his cloak. He raised his voice to stir jingling echoes from the sky of swords overhead. "Know all ye here present, that we, Ambrose, King of Chivial and Nostrimia, Prince of Nythia, do hereby raise our trusty and well-beloved Stalwart, member of the Order of the White Star, to the rank of companion in the said—" Renewed cheering drowned out the rest.

The King chuckled. The only person in Ironhall not making a noise was Stalwart himself. He was speechless. *Companion* in the White Star? Like Roland? He was going to be hobnobbing with the Chancellor, royal dukes. . . .

About to pin the badge on Stalwart's chest, Ambrose paused, as if having second thoughts. "You do realize," he muttered, almost inaudible under the tumult, "that this probably makes you the premier commoner in the land? I'll have to ask the heralds, but I do believe you'll even outrank the Speaker of the House."

"Your Majesty is being very generous," Stalwart said hoarsely.

The piggy little eyes twinkled. "Well, I couldn't be generous if I were dead. There!" And, as Stalwart was about to rise— "One other thing."

"Sire?"

"We promise to stop making jokes about the King's Daggers."

Aftermath

SERVIAN, HAVING BEEN OFFICIALLY EXPELLED, was last seen begging a carter to give him a ride into Torwell, where he could hope to find work in the lead mines.

The assassin's horse recovered from its trance, and when Ambrose left Ironhall a couple of days later, Stalwart rode it down to Blackwater. Lumpkin was there, having found his own way home safely—although he never let anyone ride him on Starkmoor again. Stalwart rode Yikes from Blackwater to Holmgarth, where she was reunited with Sheriff Sherwin.

Wart persuaded Sherwin to show Emerald his magic whistle, but Emerald said she couldn't find any magic on it, which was very strange, because it would still alarm dogs and horses, and yet it made no noise at all.

The hard part of that whole journey back to Grandon was being a royal favorite, expected to remain in close attendance on the King. Stalwart would have much preferred to ride beside Emerald, but most of the Royal Guard had that very same idea. Sir Fury was there first, though, glaring murder at any other man who came close. Since Sister Emerald did not seem to mind, he was allowed to get away with this . . . for the time being, anyway. . . .

Dave Duncan's tales of sword and sorcery are not to be missed:

SIR STALWART:
BOOK ONE OF THE KING'S DAGGERS

When Stalwart is expelled from the academy for King's Blades, he and Emerald, a former White Sister, are commanded to uncover a plot to assassinate the king. Sworn but not bound, will Stalwart succeed . . . and live?

THE CROOKED HOUSE:
BOOK TWO OF THE KING'S DAGGERS

There is evil lurking at the heart of the king's chambers, and Sir Stalwart and Sister Emerald are dispatched to investigate—only to be betrayed by one in their company.

THE TALES OF THE KING'S BLADES

THE GILDED CHAIN

Bound to absolute loyalty by a magical ritual, the King's Blades are the finest swordsmen in all Chivial, and Sir Durendal the finest of the King's Blades. But destiny has other ideas for the young knight. . . .

LORD OF THE FIRE LANDS

No candidate for the King's Blades has ever refused to serve his king. When Raider and Wasp spurn the royal honor, they must undertake a deadly journey into the dreaded Fire Lands.

SKY OF SWORDS

Princess Malinda never wanted the throne, but when treason and betrayal wrack the kingdom, only she and the Blades of the Royal Guard can save Chivial.

www.daveduncan.com